STRAIGHT FROM THE HORSE'S MOUTH

OTHER PRESS
NEW YORK

Straight

from the

Horse's Mouth

Meryem Alaoui

Translated from the French by Emma Ramadan

Originally published in French as *La vérité sort
de la bouche du cheval* in 2018 by Éditions Gallimard, Paris
Copyright © Éditions Gallimard, 2018
Translation copyright © Emma Ramadan, 2020

Production editor: Yvonne E. Cárdenas
Text designer: Jennifer Daddio
This book was set in Cochin and Charme by
Alpha Design & Composition of Pittsfield, NH

1 3 5 7 9 10 8 6 4 2

Library of Congress Cataloging-in-Publication Data

Names: Alaoui, Meryem, author. | Ramadan, Emma, translator.
Title: Straight from the horse's mouth : a novel / Meryem Alaoui ;
translated from the French by Emma Ramadan.
Other titles: Vérité sort de la bouche du cheval. English
Description: New York : Other Press, 2020. | "Originally published
in French as La vérité sort de la bouche du cheval in 2018 by
Éditions Gallimard, Paris."
Identifiers: LCCN 2020001340 (print) | LCCN 2020001341 (ebook) |
ISBN 9781892746795 (paperback) | ISBN 9781892746788 (ebook)
Subjects: LCSH: Prostitutes—Morocco—Casablanca—Fiction. |
Casablanca (Morocco)—Fiction.
Classification: LCC PQ3989.3.A73515 V4713 2018 (print) |
LCC PQ3989.3.A73515 (ebook) | DDC 843/.92—dc23
LC record available at https://lccn.loc.gov/2020001340
LC ebook record available at https://lccn.loc.gov/2020001341

2010

June

CASABLANCA, FRIDAY THE 11TH

When I'm finished working, I don't waste any time. I put my djellaba back on, smooth out its creases, and I wait. For the guy to zip up his fly, smoke a cigarette, and leave, so I can go back to my spot and harpoon another guy. That's the first thing I told Halima when she arrived last week.

The day he brought her, Houcine asked me to teach her a few things about the profession, explaining that she had just gotten out of prison. I don't know anything else about her.

And to be honest, Houcine was a little annoyed that day. So I didn't ask too many questions. He's always on edge. You can tell by his muscles. Slender but conspicuous, like they've been outlined with a pen. The last time he blew a fuse was only two days earlier. I don't remember exactly what happened. Someone he doesn't like must have disrespected one of his girls.

That's the thing he hates most in the world, who knows why. When it happens, you can't do anything to stop it. His mustache starts to quiver, he stands up straight, though he's already tall, his skin blackens, though he's already dark, and all you can see are the scars spread over his body like the cracks in the city's sidewalks. Or maybe more like the stripes on a tiger's coat. It's intimidating, and that's why we work for him. We feel safe.

Now, Halima and I, we're sitting on my bed, in the dark, and to tell you the truth, I'm only explaining the bare minimum to her. It took me years to learn what I know; I'm not about to give everything away to some slut who's just starting out. And as for Houcine—worked up or not—he doesn't get to tell me how to spend my free time.

When she arrived, there was no need to show her around my place. The tour doesn't take long. The room is rectangular, and inside are two mattresses perpendicular to the door. Lounge furniture during the day, and at night they're beds. There's one for my daughter and one for me.

I also have a small round wooden table to eat on. And an armoire for our clothes. Halima stows her things in a horrible blue bag and sleeps on a foam mattress that she brought with her. When she wakes up in the morning, she rolls it up and wedges it between the armoire and the mattress on the right.

Above one of these mattresses, there's a window that looks out onto the street. I spend a decent amount of time there. Because when I'm not watching television, I'm watching the people come and go while I eat pepitas.*

To the left of the entrance, there's a kitchen. Not a real kitchen. It's just a room that serves as a kitchen. I furnished it with a small fridge, a butane stove, a cooking pot, some large plastic tubs, and my favorite thing in the house besides the TV: a beige teapot with a pink flower on it and clear glasses, engraved with flowers, all of which sit on a round tray. I keep the tray on a wooden shelf way up high, so that nothing breaks. Opposite the shelf, there's a square opening that looks onto the hallway with the rooms rented by the other girls, and the bathroom, which has a toilet and a faucet for our ablutions.

This is my home.

And since there's no bathtub, once a week—Monday—I go to the hammam. Before going to the bath, I wash my clothes and lay them on the roof, on the wire clotheslines we share with the others in the building. I told Halima not to touch the ones all the way to the right. They belong to the neighbor

---

* Terms and phrases followed by an asterisk are defined in a glossary that begins on page 283.

on the second floor. She's not one of us, but believe me, she knows how to command respect.

The other day, we wanted to move the garbage can down below, at the entrance, because someone pointed out that when we bring men back, sometimes they grimace when they see all the black bags under the staircase. It's true that it's not very clean. Plus, when they're not closed properly, they attract street cats, who come and scavenge around inside. They rip open the bags and then garbage ends up everywhere. On the stairs, on the ground, even on the walls.

So, since we were sick of it, we sent Rabia, who lives on the first floor, to knock on everyone's door and tell them that from now on, they had to throw their trash in the large green garbage can on the sidewalk opposite the building. Not the one at the entrance. The neighbor on the second floor nearly gouged Rabia's eyes out when she heard that. Rabia, in typical Rabia fashion, was terrified.

Honestly, I get why. You'd have to see her, the neighbor, to really understand what I mean. She's tall and looks like an armoire. She has black hair, pulled back beneath her scarf. Her enormous breasts are an extension of her stomach, or the other way around. And when she speaks, she always has one eyebrow raised and her hands on her hips. As soon as you see her, you ask yourself what the hell you're doing in front of her.

So, when Rabia went to talk to her about the garbage, she was polite.

"Salaam," Rabia said to her.

"Salaam," she replied, stressing the "s" like a snake, her eyebrow prepared for war.

"My sister, please, we're having problems with the trash, so we've decided to start putting it on the opposite sidewalk, in the green garbage can. Can you put yours over there too?"

"My trash?"

And she continued without pausing for breath:

"What do you mean, my trash? You think *I'm* the one you need to tell to throw her trash in the street?"

"..."

"And you come into my home to say this to me?"

"..."

"You should take care of the filth that you all spread around here before coming to see me!"

When she started her tirade, her right hand was on her hip and her forehead closed the gap with Rabia's, like the Eid sheep when you try to catch it. When she was talking about herself, she brought her left index finger to her chest, tapping on it. And when she was talking about us, she brought it right in front of Rabia's eyes. Rabia didn't push back, even though it's not like her to miss an opportunity to stand up for herself. She just muttered, "All right, all right, no need to get worked up."

Rabia turned back around while her neighbor continued to grumble behind her back, saying, "It just keeps getting better..." From where I was on the stairs, I could see her shooting daggers into Rabia's back as she tied up her hair, pin in her mouth and head slightly cocked back to better arrange her bun. I could see her dirty look as she continued to whistle between her teeth, "And she came into my home to say this to me..."

When Rabia told us later that she hadn't wanted to fight back, we understood that it wasn't worth pushing. Because Rabia has good instincts. That's saved her more than a few times in her life. Really, we all have good instincts. And that's why we're here, in the middle of downtown Casablanca with Houcine, and not in prison or living on the streets.

Since that day, we've stopped asking Fatty for anything. That's what we call the neighbor. Fatty, or Okraïcha,* it depends. And we move the trash ourselves, since she still leaves it in the entryway.

Telling this to Halima, I might have forgotten to mention that some nights, when we're good and tipsy, we climb onto the roof, we throw Okraïcha's sheets to the ground, and we hose them down with you know what, laughing like lunatics.

In those moments, I let out a youyou like no one's ever heard before. I'm incredible at youyous. When

I unleash my tongue, it takes off like a high-speed train.

So with all the noise we make, it's impossible for Fatty not to hear us. That's part of the reason we revel in it so much.

She never comes up, never says anything.

"So, while you're in my home, you don't go anywhere near Fatty, understand?" I say to Halima.

With her distressed face and her puppy dog eyes, she says yes.

I approach the ashtray, I light a cigarette, and I puff on it rapidly as I continue to tell her about my days, emphasizing what's essential: quantity. Because you have to get with them, men, to live. At least six per day. Seven or eight is better, but six is pretty good.

When I finish with a client, I run back to my spot. Really I walk, but when you see me, it looks like I'm running. That moron Hamid, the security guard for the Majestic garage at the end of the street, told me that. The bony guy who spends his days shooing flies. He's worked in the garage for at least ten years. Since the day he failed his bac,* actually. And for ten years, he's been shooing away flies. At night, he's always hanging around with two or three of his friends, a band of bums, and he tells them everything he sees during the day.

I've never slept with any of them. In the neighborhood, I only sleep with those passing through, not anyone who lives or works here. They respect you more that way.

At least, that's my official story, because when I need to, I do it in a corner and don't tell a soul. But I've never been with Hamid. I just hang around with Hamid from time to time, so he'll tell me the latest news of the neighborhood.

Since the garage is next door to our building, I often walk by. And it's true that I always walk quickly, except when I'm looking for a man, because then you still have to look attractive. When that's on my mind, I slow down and I try to look good. I sway my hips slowly, I look right and left; I lean on my left leg, then on my right, like a camel. From behind, it's a slow, nervous movement; my butt cheeks rise and fall in jerks. It's appetizing, like the caramel puddings I buy for my daughter.

In the street, I have my spot on the sidewalk, on the stairs, near the traffic light. At the intersection of two main streets next to the market. It's the best spot. I'm not the only one there, of course, but it's the best spot.

When you're experienced, that's where Houcine puts you. Because when you have years of hard work behind you, you deserve not to struggle so much, but also because you have to know how to look out for the cops. Generally, we don't have problems with them. Houcine knows them well. And we do too...

But every now and then, they show up. Like when Anissa, the crazy girl who often hangs around the neighborhood, is off her head and screaming at the top of her lungs about God, her pussy, and the son of a bitch who did this to her all in the same breath. When they arrive, you recognize them from a distance. And even if you don't see them, you know, because one of Houcine's girls always gives a signal. We never take off running. We hide first, behind a car or a garbage can. To the outside observer, it must look pretty funny. All of us crouched down, asses squeezed in the djellabas clinging to us. Just our heads poking out. Since there are several of us, heads peak out from everywhere, like the flowers in the bouquets of old Haj, the market florist.

Then, we wait to see what will happen. Because it's not always us they come for. But when they approach, we're all ready to scamper off in the same direction: our building. At the street corner, before turning left, we all stop underneath the neighborhood tree. Most of the time, it ends in a sprint, and then our heads don't look like flowers in a bouquet anymore. They're more like those decorative plastic dogs you put in cars' rear windows. Bobbing right to left, like they're on springs. Because while we run, we check to see whether the cops are following us. Sometimes, even at that stage, it's a false alarm. And then we all return to our places and relight our cigarettes.

Usually, I'm on my spot on the stairs with Samira, Rabia, and Fouzia. They're the girls who are always with me. That bitch Hajar and her girlfriend—who's just as much of a cunt—stand on the other side of the street, facing the market. During times of truce, we let them sit next to us. But most of the time, they stand opposite.

And then, we wait. For men to pass so we can put ideas in their heads. When they're near us, we sigh. That way, if they want, they stop, they get out of their cars and they say something like, "Have we met, beautiful?" Well, to be honest, they rarely get out of their cars. However, when they walk by on foot, we never miss them. They act like they're just passing through but it's a load of bullshit. They come for us and we know it.

Sunday is the best day of the week, better than Saturday night, better than Friday night, better than any other day. The men who've had difficult weeks come to see us. They spend the afternoon in one of the local bars, and when they leave, around four or five o'clock, after several Storks or Spéciales, life seems good. They have just one desire: to make the pleasure and the oblivion last. And they do it inside us. It doesn't last long, but it's something.

So when they pass by in the street, they say, "Do we know each other, beautiful?" Then, you negotiate. Not for long, because they know our rates. I get a thousand to a thousand six hundred rials* a pop.

I never extend credit, not like that slut Hajar, who undercuts the market. When you're done negotiating, you walk past the guy for a few yards, and he follows you. As you go, you look back every now and then to make sure he's still there and to keep his interest piqued.

When a man follows me and I'm concentrating on how I move, I can feel the pressure of his hard-on between my butt cheeks. I show them that I want them because in general, men like that. And we like when they're happy because then they pay without making a fuss.

And I know what I'm talking about. I've been in this profession for nearly fifteen years now.

Today, I'm feeling chatty. But normally I don't go into the details. I simply say that my name is Jmiaa, that I'm thirty-four years old, that I have a daughter, and that to live, I use what I've got.

FRIDAY THE 18TH

Today, the street is swarming with people. A typical Friday. It's June, it's hot in Casablanca, and the days are long. At the beginning of last month, they announced on the news that they would change from winter to summer hours and they added an hour to our clock. They explained it by saying that it would save money. I think it's a good idea. Now, it's after eight-thirty and the sun is still in the sky.

I put on my red djellaba, the red scarf with green flowers, a line of kohl and a layer of red lipstick. My hair is fastened tightly. Fortunately, I didn't cut it the other day. I was angry—I don't remember why—and on a whim, I almost ruined ten years of waiting for it to reach my waist.

Now, I'll join the girls on the stairs and have a few drinks while I get going. I'm walking quickly because I'm already late. I'm carrying a black bag with a bottle of red and a plastic cup. Today, it was my turn to buy the wine. Yesterday, it was Samira's, and the day before, I don't remember whose it was.

I'm lucky to have this bottle in my hands. Earlier, I got distracted in front of the television and when I looked at the time, it was already ten to eight. Ten minutes before the liquor store closes. Now with this shitty extra summer hour, we don't realize it's so late.

It wouldn't have been the end of the world if it had been closed. But then I would have had to pay even more for a bottle from that crook Bachir, the grocer. I won't tell you how much money that guy makes selling alcohol under the table. What he charges us makes him enough to grease the palms of all the cops in the neighborhood so they'll turn a blind eye. And with how much we drink, I can tell you, there's no chance they'll regain their sight. Son of a bitch!

Anyway, just now, when I saw the time, I leapt up. I threw on my djellaba for quick errands, the one that's hanging behind the front door, and I hurtled down the three floors to the street.

I didn't bring my shadow with me to the store, she was too slow. My shadow is Halima. All she does is follow me around. I tell her come and she comes. When I say we're leaving, she leaves too. Even now, suddenly, she's behind me.

Sometimes, it annoys me that she clings to me so much. But when I turn around to tell her off for slowing me down, I'm always taken aback. She sulks so much. It's like she's carrying the weight of the world on her shoulders. So I sigh loudly, so she'll understand that she's pissing me off, and I move faster. And that moron, she hurries to keep up with me.

She's still staying at my place, and to tell you the truth, she's starting to get on my nerves. She never wants to do anything other than work. And when she's not working, she spends her time reading or listening to the Quran, with a headscarf—so old you can see her hair through it—on her head. Acting like she's a good, serious girl. If you are what you say you are, what are you doing here then?

She's never answered that question, but I don't press. Because I know from experience that in these situations, it's just a matter of time.

"Can you pick up the pace?" I say, turning toward Halima.

" . . ."

We haven't arrived at the market yet, but I can already see the girls sitting on the stairs. They're all there. Samira, Fouzia, Rabia. Even Hajar and her girlfriend. They've already found things to drink. Hajar is holding a white plastic cup to her lips. And it's the cunning Samira who's filling the glasses so she can control how much is poured.

Lately, Samira's been seeing a guy who tells her all sorts of stories, and she won't stop talking about it. This guy hit her, and then came crying back to her like a baby. He's a cop. She would never admit it, but I think she has a crush on that asshole. When he speaks, she looks at him with her mouth wide open and she hangs onto him as if he were the only man on earth.

Physically, there's nothing special about him. He's big, mustachioed, he always wears a white shirt and gray linen pants. No taller or shorter than the average guy. If you don't know him, he doesn't seem any nicer or any lousier than the others. But I don't like him. I know he's twisted on the inside. He has a vicious gaze, like the devil.

On top of that, when you look at the two of them, it's clear that she's a thousand times better than him. She's plain too. But she's curvy in the right places. And her hair is an impeccable color. At its roots, it's dark, and the farther down you go, the lighter it gets. At the bottom, her hair is almost blond. And she's not just well endowed. Samira is a real woman.

Capable. Confident. I really don't know what she's doing with that loser.

The other day, we were all at the bar over there, the Pommercy, with that freak Aziz and two of his friends, also cops. They had ordered a bottle of red. We were having a good time. The guys were in the mood to party and were telling us a bunch of stories about the precinct.

Samira went to the bathroom. As soon as she got up, he put one of his hands on my ass. Normally, he doesn't put his hands on me because Samira doesn't like when he touches other girls. And I understand that. But I left his hand where it was. I'm not crazy enough to push a cop off of me.

He was happy because in the afternoon, he had nabbed a thief, a little young thing from who knows where, and he had had his fun with him in the pit. That's what we call the hole. While Samira was in the bathroom, he kept kneading my ass, telling us how scared the kid had been when he started asking him questions.

"So, you little hooligan, what were you doing with your friend in the middle of Maârif* this afternoon?" he said to him.

"Nothing. We went for a walk," the kid replied.

"A walk? What's a peasant like you doing taking a walk in Maârif?"

With that, he grimaced to mimic the bad stench he'd sniffed as he got nearer to the kid's face.

"What were you doing there, huh?"

"Nothing, we were walking," the young guy repeated.

That was all it took for Aziz to lose it. The guy he'd caught red-handed was acting all innocent, hoping he would get off. He and his friend had hopped on a motorcycle and gone to Maârif to steal a few bags as they drove around. He was the one driving. They approached a woman in her fifties, who was walking in front of them on the sidewalk. His friend got off, ran up to the lady, grabbed her bag, and hopped back on the motorcycle. Nothing abnormal about that. Except that they were unlucky. The police car was right on the street corner. As soon as they saw the car, they tossed their prize. But they were caught like a couple of idiots. And like idiots, they tried to deny that it was them.

Since their luck was really rotten that day, they found themselves confronted by Aziz, Samira's cop. Who couldn't wait for a guy more pathetic than he was himself to fall into his lap. While Aziz was recounting the story, he was reveling in it. The more the kid tried to protect his face, the more Aziz slapped him. A real rabid dog! And as he told the story, he was howling with laughter.

When Samira returned, she saw Aziz had his arm around me. She said nothing and simply sat down next to him. She was irritated. But Samira's not stupid. She acted like any other intelligent girl would have done. She took a cigarette, turned toward him to ask for a light, and pressed her breasts against his chest.

He forgot all about my ass. Probably because he knows what's under Samira's djellaba.

And that's when he said to her, "And I'm here at the end of the day with a bombshell in my arms, isn't that right, beautiful?" And turning toward his friends, he said: "Look how beautiful she is, how often do you see girls like this?"

Samira roared with laughter, his friends chuckled, and I did the same. And then we ordered another round.

All that is to say that when I show up at the stairs with Halima, Samira is talking shit about Aziz to Hajar.

"That son of a bitch, he thinks I have nothing better to do than wait around for him. But guys like him are a dime a dozen. I'll show him, that motherfucker."

I sit down, I light a Marvel, and I listen out of one ear as I wait for them to change the subject. I'm sick of Aziz. At the beginning, I was willing to give advice, I told Samira what she should do to quit arguing with him, but I gave up because she never listens. It's always the same story: she says that she's going to stop seeing him and that she's going to get rid of him. And every time we're at the bar and he shows up, she runs to him. I've always told her that for him, a pussy is a pussy, and hers is wide open so there's no reason for him to try to find another. But talking to Samira is like pouring water into sand.

"Jmiaa, what are you doing?"

Rabia is staring at me. She's standing there with a cigarette in her hand and a grimace on her face.

"What are you doing?" she repeats.

I look at her and I look around me.

To my left, on the sidewalk, is Robio.* I hadn't noticed him. Robio is a guy who sells hangers, thingamajigs to make cars smell good, and other junk. I know him well. He comes by often. He sells his trash near the light, next to the tree. His merchandise changes all the time, according to availability and what he manages to buy with the two pennies he has in assets. Sometimes he has socks or toys for children. So I buy things for my daughter.

He must have been there for a while, looking at me, waiting for me to get up. And so I do, but honestly, I'm not very motivated. He's wearing glasses—thick like the bottom of a bottle—he has an eye that's always staring off to the left, hair of an inexplicable color, somewhere between brown and red, and the breath of a corpse.

I get up, my right hand on my hip to help me stand. It's clear that I don't really want to, but I make an effort. He's a regular client. I'm the one he always seeks out before turning to Fouzia, then Hajar.

I look at him and I smile. I'm about to leave, about to walk past for him to follow me. I turn to look at Fouzia and I cross my eyes and stick out my tongue to imitate the redhead. Just to make her laugh. He doesn't see anything because he's on the opposite side. She bursts out laughing, and I smile while holding back a fit of giggles. I overtake him and walk toward the building.

We're in front of my room. My daughter is there. That old lady Mina decided today of all days to go to the village. Do I pay her to watch my daughter or to buy bus tickets, that shithead?

Samia watches us enter, she gets up from her mattress.

"Did you eat?" I ask.

"No, not yet," she responds.

"When did Mina bring you back?"

"I don't know. Not long ago."

Behind me, Robio is getting agitated. I have to speed this up.

"Go outside. Robio has to repair something," I say to Samia.

It's very rare that she's there when I bring men home, but when she is, I tell her that they're repairmen. For the wooden furniture, the television, the fridge, the windows...whatever.

I don't know what she thinks, but what's certain is that she's growing up and if this continues, it might start to cause some problems.

"I'll be right there, it won't take long," I continue, handing her a wooden stool to sit on and signaling to four-eyes with the other hand for him to get himself ready.

I close the door. Let's go, on the mattress. Pull down your boxers, lay me on my back, lift my djellaba. He's a two-pump chump. It won't take long. With Samia outside, I'm happy it's him and not someone else. The problem with this line of work is that you never know who you'll end up with. It's not worth it for me to go into the details or to recount everything I see. But let's just say that I've come across everything you can imagine and things you wouldn't even want to think about.

The guy who wants you to devour him, holding onto your neck like it's the last thing on earth. Drowning in a raging sea, he suffocates you in his flabby flesh and wants you to swallow for him. In his shipwreck, you are the raft. Neither flesh nor blood nor liver. Back on land, he leaves you on the briny bank—foaming and filthy. And the tide takes you again.

Another.

This guy is furious. He needs to empty his vigor in a long, hard jet into everyone he meets. Your ass is his due. The overzealous cop charges, he kicks, hits and tears your shoulder. In this field, where he sees a crowd cheering for him, his hands whip you like the air whipped up while he's racing. When he's done, his menacing eye challenges the earth over which he is the master. But once he's ejected his sticky glory into you, the illusion transforms into hatred. So he hits you, because he is only himself. Tortured, drunk, and alone.

And another.

Who transfers filth from girl to girl, room to room. He skips the latex, preferring the yellowed streaks that he leaves behind, the better to find them—still warm—inside of another. In the haze of alcohol, you gave in without a second thought. But the night doesn't play favorites, and as you scratch until you bleed, you're afraid. And in the morning you wash everything, and you move on to something else.

A few bills smoothed out by an uncertain hand.

The kid who delivers them wants to leave his innocence and his cheeks, turning red, behind the door. The stories he told his friends are no longer enough to make him a man. He tries to puff up his chest, his lips tremble beneath some peach fuzz, his tongue is dried up by fear. You watch his attempts to gather himself. You want to tell him that there's no going back after this. But you keep quiet. You even help him to slide in, to shed the peace that encumbers him.

You straddle all of them. The loser, the frustrated guy, the lonely guy, the son of a whore, the one just passing through.

The one who blames the warmth of your hand for his weak, sterile joy.

And the one for whom no hole satisfies his hatred. Who is not appeased until he hears the ripping sound of a brown and bloody stain.

And the one who pumps his useless sweat into your stomach. He has been cursed never to eat his fill, so he bites your flesh. So that his teeth—today at least—serve some purpose. And in the wheeze of his sulfur breath, he spurts his bitterness onto your cheek and your tangled hair.

And then there's the guy who drowns his shame in drink every day and who—when night comes—makes you vomit your own, in dirty toilets and with the excuse of contaminated wine.

But, in the end, you don't give a shit about them, their misery and their grime. Because you know that's just how it is. And that on this earth, everyone has their lot.

And so, in the shitty grab bag of fate, I feel simply blessed when I get a quick one.

Like this Robio, who looks at me while pulling up his pants, which he had hardly lowered, and says, "What was she laughing at, your whore friend earlier?"

"You know her, she's an idiot, you know she laughs at anything," I answer in a detached voice.

He settles for that response, but I know he's bothered. When he goes back there with a few glasses of wine in him, it'll turn sour between them.

He zips up his fly and takes a bill out of his pocket. I stand, pull up my underwear, lower my djellaba, and follow him.

My daughter is sitting with her back to the wall. She's waiting for us to leave so she can return to her cartoons.

"Thank you for coming," I say.

Robio stares at me and eventually responds, with a crooked smile, "Whenever you like."

I signal for Samia to enter. My daughter is like me when I was her age. I was thin like a gazelle, with straight black hair. She seems tiny and dainty in this hallway. I want to take her in my arms and eat her up. But I still have the guy's smell on my face.

*I*t's night now. I made dinner for Samia—two eggs with olive oil and cumin—and I left. When I arrived at the stairs, the girls were no longer at the market.

I find them at the Pommercy. I'm at the entrance, and the curtain of green and yellow beads hanging there is disgustingly filthy. The pig manager doesn't use sanicroix* to wash the floor, and she hardly rinses the glasses before putting them back under the counter. So you can imagine the state of the curtain.

Fuck, no! Chaïba! Chaïba is here! His giant mouth is twisted with laughter behind a good dozen empty Spéciale bottles and an enormous belly. I don't know why I want to bury my tongue in it. It's not that he's all that good-looking or anything. He just has that effect on me, I can't help it. Bouchaïb is the only guy I sleep with who has that effect on me, and he's the only one whose name—Chaïba—leaves a nice taste in my mouth.

But I have no desire to talk to him today. We saw each other barely a week ago and there's no way I can find myself involved yet again in a situation where I start to develop feelings.

I turn slowly toward the door to leave, without letting my djellaba swish, without a sound, lowering my head. Please let no one notice me, please let no one notice me, please let no one notice me...

"Jmiaa! My beauty! We haven't even said hello and you're leaving already?" he yells from behind his table, in my direction. His voice is so loud that from where I am, and even with my back to him, I feel the beers in front of him tremble.

I stop. I turn. I flash a fake smile, all the way to my ears, and I say, as if I hadn't seen him, "Chaïba! Is that you?"

"Come here, beauty. I've been waiting for you since noon. Where've you been?"

"Here and there, out and about. Where did you think? And you, where've you been?"

"Me? Nowhere special. Come, sit with us."

He's at a table with his two friends who work for him—Belaïd and Saïd. I walk slowly toward them, skirting the tables and pushing aside the empty chairs in front of me. I approach him, he stands up and kisses my hand while bowing very low, as if we were in a film. He squeezes me in his arms so tight that I'm lifted off the floor, and he orders another round for the table.

I take a sip of beer from the bottle in front of him while I wait for my own. I like beer. Red wine is good too, but beer is better. It fizzes in the mouth like lemon soda, and it smells good. There's a song by Abdel Halim* playing in the background.

We down the Spéciales, one after another. The bar starts to fill up. I see the girls, each with her guy, except Halima. She's at the corner of a table where everyone is laughing, and she's sitting with an empty stare in front of a Coke. Moron!

Chaïba orders more beers as soon as they're empty. He leans toward me and says, "A trip to Jdida,* what do you think?"

*H*onestly, I hesitated before saying yes. But in the end, you only have one life. What's the point of filling it with nothing?

I'm sitting in the front of the car, next to Bou-chaïb and his enormous belly. Belaïd and Saïd are in the back. Chaïba must have an important business transaction to see to if he's bringing the two of them. The sound of the slamming car doors resounds in my head. There's no one outside except for two bums vegetating at the foot of a tree. It's bizarre. This street, I know it well but it's as if I were seeing it for the first time.

The buildings, gray and grimy during the day, are nearly orange in the glow of the streetlights. The cars parked in the lot are silently aligned. No movement, no yells, no cars fighting over who has the right-of-way, no bicycle about to knock you over. There's no beggar half-fallen into the trash, no mothers selling fish alongside the street vendors, no one selling fruit, no children coming back from school stopping for a Dannon. There are also no sellers of pepitas or mattresses or thimbles. There's nothing. Nothing but a single cat crossing the street, taking its time, without fear of anyone yanking its tail.

I buckle my seat belt. Bouchaïb pulls on it to be sure it's fastened, and he grabs my breast in passing while continuing to look at me with the smile of someone who is very hungry and who has just been served a roasted rack of lamb, coated with butter and sprinkled with cumin. He raises his left eyebrow, makes a little movement of his head downward, in the direction of his thingamajig, which is all swollen.

I giggle and place my left hand on his backrest, wedging myself into my seat. In front of me, the road is clear.

The gold bracelets on my wrist knock against each other. He caresses my hand and tickles me between my thighs.

"Let's go, *anafa!** Bouchaïb says, shifting into first gear.

Again I make my bracelets jingle and with my mouth wide like a gaping wallet—as Samira says—I repeat after him:

"*Anafa!*"

His associates are slumped on their seats; they laugh and we take off at full speed.

I don't know why we're giggling, but I can't stop laughing, a deep belly laugh. It's hot, fat, it fills the space, like my arms, like my stomach, like my breasts, like me on the seat. I feel like I'm swelling, filling the passenger side.

"Are you happy, beautiful?"

Bouchaïb smiles at me again with his unending mouth.

"What makes you say that?" I respond with a grimace.

I can't stand when he's pleased with himself. He doesn't respond—probably because he's not in the mood to argue—and turns toward Saïd, saying, "Pass the Spéciales."

Saïd leans toward a gray canvas bag at his feet and hands Bouchaïb a beer.

"What, she's not good enough for one?" he asks, nodding toward me.

Saïd leans over again and passes me a beer. I take it and I pull out the Marvels from my bra. The packet is a bit crumpled. I pull out a cigarette, smooth it, and light it.

We drive fast along the coast, the music blasting. I can't remember the last time I went on a drive like this. It must have been a long time ago, or else I'm too drunk to remember.

Chaïba stops at a gas station to buy cigarettes. He leaves the car stereo on with the cassette running. It's Haja El Hamdaouia.* I stay in the car, and his friends get out to piss, laughing and singing like lunatics. They undo their belts while moving their butts to the rhythm of the music.

"Stop, you're spraying me," Saïd says.

"*Ba Lahcen bechouia, ha aha bechouia,**" Belaïd says, ignoring him, swaying his hips to the rhythm of the music, his arms horizontal.

His liberated cock moves like him from right to left and from back to front. He sprays piss everywhere. On his pants, on Saïd (who shouts), and on the tall grass in front of them. Bouchaïb comes back and lines up next to them. He has a cigarette dangling from his lips.

When he takes a drag, he frowns, his lips pursed forward, the cigarette hanging slightly to the left and his mouth twisted slightly to the right. His neck is taut, bending backward.

"What's up with you, Chaïba? Sick of your life?" Belaïd says, imitating him.

"Such an ass!" Bouchaïb responds, turning his body as if he were going to spray him.

Saïd distracts them. "Wanna bet that I can hit that rock?"

And all three of them take aim at the large rock in front of them. Belaïd tries, but he's got no more in him, so he pulls back up his pants and with a loud "ptooey!" sends a big gob of spit onto the rock. "Can you aim like that?"

Challenge accepted! All three spit toward the rock. I clap my hands to the music to encourage them.

Our racket accentuates how deserted the station is. But the only two customers, drinking their coffee at a table, smoking a cigarette in the dingy light, don't give a damn. They turn their heads toward us, continuing to puff on their cigarettes without saying a word. Neither to each other nor to tell us to shut up.

The calm of that vision suddenly enshrouds us, and we get back on the road.

We arrive at Jdida fairly quickly. It's late. We drive along the cliff. We pass a few intersections, we turn down streets that all look the same, and we stop at the foot of a house. A guy, only his silhouette visible, comes out and gives us the keys to the apartment where we'll sleep.

I'm tired. I've had a lot to drink. Bouchaïb and I do something that resembles fucking. It's hazy. It's lethargic. He eventually finishes. About time.

Now, he's snoring with his mouth wide open, lying on his back, fully dressed, with his stomach extended to the sky.

My head is spinning, the ceiling drops closer, grows distant, becomes a blur. I think I'm going to puke.

SATURDAY THE 19TH

It's already morning. I'm in a complete daze. I had my breakfast in a café at the end of the street where we stayed. I ate alone. I don't know where the others went. A work thing, probably.

Before going out, I called Samira to tell her to keep an eye on Samia. I don't trust Halima very much.

Today, the sun is a bit cold. Even though it's summer. It must not be very late. There's still fog, and few people out and about. I'm sitting on a low white wall that runs along the beach. I have my back to the sea because all that water makes me dizzy.

It's always been that way, since the first time I laid eyes on it. That was a long time ago. I was twenty years old and had just arrived in Casa. I was beautiful! Fresh as a rose, let me tell you. Now, you see me like this, a bit tired, but you should have seen me in my youth. I had big eyes, long eyelashes. My eyes were shiny, soft, deep as a well. And black. In my neighborhood, they said that I had the eyes of a cow they were so beautiful. And my hair was thick, like a horse's tail. And my chest went out to the sky it was so proud. Let me tell you.

At that time, my husband was still around, and he's the one who brought me to the sea. It was in Aïn Diab,* I remember it well. It was a Sunday, early in our marriage.

It was the first time I had seen something so big and boundless. Even fields aren't like that. There are always hills or a tree or a stable that blocks your view. The sea was gigantic, and seeing the line where sky and sea touch, I immediately thought that that was the place where you climb to the sky to reach paradise.

My husband made fun of me for a long time; every time he wanted to take me to the beach, he would turn to me and say, "Hey, Jmiaa, a quick trip to paradise, what do you say?"

When he brought me there, as soon as my feet touched the sea, I don't know what took hold of me. I started to run, run, run on the sand like a horse. It was as if a fire had been lit under my feet. When I stopped and looked up, the world spun. I was scared for my life because I didn't know if it would ever stop or not. I would spin so much that I would fall, right on my horse's ass. I wasn't fat then like I am now. I was simply round and firm. My husband couldn't stop laughing.

Since that day, I get vertigo when I spend too much time staring at the sea.

And this breakfast I just ate, I'm not sure it was such a good idea. I have heartburn.

Choufi ghirou, a l'azara 'ata Allah, choufi ghirou.
My telephone is ringing!

It's Chaïba: "Hello, where are you?"

"I'm around. What about you?" I said, using the casual voice of someone who's around.

"I'm waiting for you at the apartment. Come."

I arrive at the apartment. Bouchaïb is already there, without the others. I feel no desire right now, especially not with the dizziness, but I like Chaïba. I approach him with a big smile, asking him, "Are you itching down here?" I caress the bulge in his pants.

I won't get too graphic, but it's not just a bulge he has down there; it's a mountain. We head to the bedroom.

This morning, I hadn't noticed that the hallway was green.

Bouchaïb grabs my chest. I know that's the part of me he likes the most. And my ass. I stand on my tiptoes and I press my breasts against his torso. My hand opens his shirt. His hairs slide between my fingers. He likes that too. I even pull on them a little.

Beneath his mustache, he's smiling from ear to ear. He's already worked up. "You missed me, huh," he says.

And he adds, "None of those other losers fuck you like I do, huh?"

He talks as he sucks on my face with his lips, which seem enormous to me now. If he keeps going like this, he'll end up eating me. I'll disappear into that chasm where all his rotten teeth went.

"And their dicks, what are they like?"

He leads me toward the bed. He crushes me with all his weight. Between his stomach and mine, there's a lot of fat. Bouchaïb likes to spread me like a sheet and stretch out over me. He's lucky I've got some cushion to me. But it's not unpleasant. His large palms lift my djellaba, climb along my underwear, pressing down on my thighs. He lowers my underwear, barely unzips his pants, takes out his whatchamacallit and enters, wriggling to get inside.

"Is that what you wanted? Did you miss my cock, huh?"

Fuck, why does this asshole keep saying "huh"? What does he want me to say? Yours is the biggest, the sweetest, and the most delicious dick I've ever had, is that it? What is it with guys' obsession with their dicks?

He moves faster. His hands don't know what to grab onto anymore. My breasts, my ass, my stomach, my chin, and my lips.

Old Mina said to me one day, "They don't pay you to understand. Remember one thing: if the dick's aroused, the mind's in the clouds." And she was right. He wants me to tell him he's the best? No problem.

But Bouchaïb doesn't really want me to answer. He wants me to make noise. Instead of talking, I make the sound of a cow giving birth. That's his favorite.

"Mmmmmmoooh."

"Hee-haw," he responds.

Bouchaïb has just brayed. He's happy and I see all of his teeth. He's lying on the bed and I'm at his side. The ceiling is white and the sheets beneath my hands are wrinkled and rigid.

My hiked-up djellaba makes a cushion for the top of my butt. I pull on the underwear that's stuck below my knees while he keeps staring at the light bulb hanging from the ceiling, his mouth agape.

I never know what to do when Chaïba and I finish. If I get up, I'm afraid it'll remind him that I do this all day. If I speak, it ruins the ambiance.

He takes his phone and dials a number. It rings.

"Hello, Saïd? Come and get me. I'll wait for you at the apartment."

He's taken care of my problem without even knowing it. I'm free to get up.

Said and Belaïd came to get us and now we're in a bar I've been to several times before. Every time with Bouchaïb. It's on the way out of Jdida. There's a terrace as big as the sea opposite us, and at the end of the day, the sun sets directly across from the bar. As if you had ordered it off the menu.

Apart from that, the tables and chairs are ordinary. Bouchaïb always sits in the same spot. In the corner, to the left of the entrance, in a space where there's only room for one big round table. Between the wooden bar and the enormous windows with the blue frames, overlooking the sea. All the decoration comes from the homes of fishermen. To make sure you know we're at the beach. That kind of thing. I don't see how pieces of boats and nets qualify as decoration but if that's the boss's thing, why not?

Chaïba has a business meeting with some people. As soon as we arrived, the boss recognized him and approached us.

"Bouchaïb, it's been so long!" he said to him, giving him a big smooch on the cheek. "All's well? Family's good? Kids are good? Welcome," he says, placing one hand behind his back and motioning with the other toward the room to invite him in.

He didn't even glance at the rest of us. He acted as if Saïd, Belaïd, and I weren't there. I don't care. Besides, I ignored him too. I lit a cigarette and waited for them to finish their greetings and for the boss to bring us to our table.

Since then, I've been downing beers. One after the other. I don't know how many I've had. The sun set a little while ago.

Bouchaïb is sitting with a guy in a brown djellaba who wants to sell him a piece of land that's not exactly aboveboard in terms of property deeds. They're negotiating the price, I think.

Belaïd and Saïd are speaking between themselves. Considering how long they've hung out together, God only knows what they still have to talk about.

Lots of people come and go from the bar. There are a few faces I recognize. Since we arrived, I haven't said a word to anyone. I'm tired. I want only one thing: for them to finish so we can leave.

While I wait, I down tapas, Marvels, and Spéciales. But despite everything I've eaten to fill my stomach, my head is still spinning. I've really been hitting the bottle too much recently. I don't think I've been sober for the last three weeks.

I see Bouchaïb but I can't manage to hear what he's saying.

He's making dramatic gestures with his arms. His mouth opens wide when he speaks. He laughs, holding his stomach. He leans on the shoulder of the real estate agent next to him. But it's like a dream.

Everything is blurry. I want to go home. I want to be in my room. To lie on my mattress and watch the television until sleep overtakes me. I'm sick of all these people.

*W*e leave. None of us speak. We exit Jdida. We pass in front of the police station on the way to Casablanca. A cop signals for us to pull over. Pain in my ass.

I put out my cigarette. I act intimidated. They like it when you're afraid.

The uniform leans over while shining his flashlight around the inside of the car to see how much he can make off of us. Three men, a whore. It reeks of alcohol. Jackpot.

"License and registration," he says, pulling a face.

As if you need to make an effort for your face to scare people, asshole!

Saïd leans over Bouchaïb's knees to open the glove compartment. He takes out a black leather pouch and hands it to the police officer with a big smile. As he gives it to him, he asks the cop how he's doing. The cop doesn't respond. He takes the papers, turns his back to him, and walks away. It's going to cost us.

Saïd waits for the cop to move a bit farther away and gets out of the car to join him.

I don't need to see the scene to describe it to you.

The cop looks at the registration, the pink permit open between his fingers. He takes out his notepad and writes up an infraction. Saïd joins him. They argue. The cop turns his head toward the other cars that he stopped farther on and who are also waiting for him. Suddenly he decides to go see them.

Saïd waits alone on the side of the road, like a rejected suitor. Finally, the cop returns, walking slowly. He says nothing and is still sulking. Saïd says something to him, laughing. The cop plays innocent, like a virgin, the hint of a smile at his lips.

Saïd unleashes his charm. He speaks, making his hands dance through the air. The virgin looks at him, encourages him, but doesn't cede. Saïd gains confidence. He speaks louder, laughs openly. The virgin relaxes. Saïd has nearly done it. He keeps going. Ingratiating but determined. The cop likes that. That's it. He acquiesces.

They barely touch, their hands graze and they consummate the act.

In the wings, no youyou rings out. Everyone knew the virgin was sewn back up.

But at least now we can go home.

We drive fast. We're all in a hurry to get there. I can't see anything out of the window, but we're going fast. Everything is black and nothing has an outline. If I hadn't already known, I wouldn't have been able to tell you the direction we were driving in.

We're already back. Maybe I fell asleep. I don't know.

Saïd stops the car at the corner of the street. There are people outside and the pepita seller is still there. It's not yet midnight.

I don't have the energy to do anything tonight. Not even talk to anyone. Not even watch television after all.

"Do you need anything?" Bouchaïb asks, to see if I want money.

"No, I'm fine," I say, opening the car door and placing my sandal on the sidewalk.

I just want to go home.

"Ciao."

They don't respond. They can all go fuck themselves.

With a bit of luck, the religious girl and Samia will be asleep. And I'll go to bed too. I've got nothing better to do at this hour.

July

SUNDAY THE 11TH

Today is the World Cup final. Spain versus the Netherlands. They're playing right now as I talk to you. To tell the truth, I don't care about the game at all, but I know it's on because the street is empty. All the neighborhood men are in the cafés and I haven't had much work for a Sunday. Their energy is focused on soccer and they don't have any left for below the belt.

You could hear the wind speak, that's how quiet it is. Like in the Western films we watched on TV when we were little. The parking lot security guard even abandoned his post and his tea tray on the sidewalk.

For now, no one has scored a goal. Even though I'm not watching the game, I know.

When someone scores a goal, you can't miss it. When it happens—you don't know where it comes from, but it's so loud that you feel it in your chest— you hear *Ilyeh!* *Ilyeh!* And the coffees spill onto the sidewalks and the men jump up and down and embrace.

Usually, when there's a match, I like to be in the street. I plop myself down on the stairs by the intersection. The men in the cafés watch soccer, and I watch them. To each his own spectacle.

But right now, I don't feel like it. And I also don't feel like staying in my bedroom with Halima and her pathetic expression, like she's always saying look at how miserable and how serious I am. Fuck off!

I'm going to hang out with Hamid. I know he'll be alone. The match doesn't air on Al Aoula or on 2M. It's too expensive, apparently. And I know his friends, faced with the choice between the match and Hamid, won't give it much thought. The jokes he tells, as good as they are, don't provide the same thrill as the World Cup final. Some friendship!

Before heading out, I had a few drinks. That moron Hamid only has tea.

From a distance, I see him lying in his wooden shed at the entrance of the garage. The shower curtain that serves as his door hangs by a nail.

Hamid is lying beneath his violet and gray covers, bingeing on TV. A boiling teapot is on the metal tray in front of him.

"You're not going to fix that table before you burn yourself?" I say to him by way of hello.

The tray is balanced on a small round table with three legs, one of which is held together with wire.

"Salaam, will you have some tea?" he answers, pointing to a glass on the shelf next to the screen.

There are several glasses and no two are the same. I take one at random and turn around to grab one of the chairs at the entrance of the shed, the ones his friends sit on when they loaf around in here.

"So, what's new with you?" he asks me, sitting up.

"You know. Nothing special," I answer, lighting a cigarette.

I don't offer him a cigarette, but I put the pack on the table. He doesn't really like cigarettes. He prefers to puff from time to time on the joints of one of his friends, the blond with the blue eyes. He doesn't like when I smoke inside, but I act like I've forgotten. Because I think it's ridiculous for him to put on airs as if we were sitting in a palace. His shack is open to the winds, he has a shower curtain instead of a door, and I can't smoke?

The images flick by on the television. The tea has a lot of honey in it, which I like. We don't speak. It's often this way with him and that's how I like it.

Sometimes we laugh and have fun, and other times, we have nothing to say and keep quiet.

"You have good timing," he says to me without taking his eyes off the screen, "I've been meaning to talk to you about something for a while now."

"Here I am."

In the street, a red car passes. It's silent, like everything around here.

"The other day, a woman who lives here, in the building right on the corner—you won't know who she is even if I describe her—came to speak to me. She's small and fat and has curly hair. She's the owner of the Honda," he says to me, indicating the blue car parked opposite us.

"Hmmm..."

"I know her. We talk from time to time, the two of us. You know how I am, I like to get to know people. She's a good lady. Her husband works in fashion. He was on the TV the other day. Anyway, I didn't really understand what she wants but she has a niece who works for a paper, or for the TV in the Netherlands, and she wanted to know if I knew one of the girls who hangs around the market because she wants to meet one of you."

"For what?" I ask, turning toward him.

He brings the tea to his mouth and looks straight ahead of him.

"I don't know. I think it's for an interview or something like that. I don't know exactly. But she told me that her niece was willing to pay just for talking."

"Is it for something in the Netherlands or here?" I ask him.

"I don't know."

"So?"

"So what?" he answers.

"So what did you say?"

"I said that I would see, what do you think I said?" he responds, throwing his covers to his feet in a gesture that's both smooth and taut at the same time—like the tongue of a chameleon—and getting up to go to the bathroom.

Why would that woman want to meet me? If it's for Moroccan TV, I could guess which show she worked for. I know every show that runs on 2M and on Al Aoula. I never miss a program, not a single one slips through my fingers. If there's one thing I know about, it's shows. I'm an expert on all of them.

"Since I forgot to talk to you about it, she asked me again yesterday or the day before," he yelled from the bathroom.

I can tell you who acted in what and when and the name of the first stepmother of the hero in a series. But when it comes to the Netherlands, I have no way of knowing what she wants.

Hamid comes back. He's standing at the door with half of the beige shower curtain on his head.

He dries his hands on his jeans. I ask him, "What do you think?"

"I have no idea, but maybe there's a bit of money to be made, no?"

"Is it for a paper or for the television?"

It gives me a headache not knowing what it is she wants.

"I told you that I don't know anything, but how about this, I'll ask her and I'll tell you what it's all about, okay?" he responds, shoving his hands back in his pockets.

WEDNESDAY THE 14TH

Since that conversation with Hamid the other day, nothing special has happened. The day before yesterday, I tried to speak to him to get an update, but he didn't respond, that ass. And again yesterday, I passed in front of the garage. He was with people and he acted like he didn't see me when I waved to him from the other side of the road.

In the meantime I've been thinking of a way to do that dick a favor and do his shitty interview without anyone recognizing me.

I told myself that if this girl works for television, I'll ask them to use a square that blurs my face. So that people don't recognize me. Like in *Moukhtafoune.**

But if it's a newspaper or a book, I'm not interested. I don't like reading. You read a book, you bust your ass trying to decipher it, you have to use your imagination, you can't hear the characters' voices, you don't know if they're good-looking or not. To tell you the truth, I've never read one, but I know that it's a chore.

You see, I racked my brain with all this thinking, and he disappears just like that.

I didn't try to call to him again. He can go fuck himself! And the Dutchwoman too, for that matter. If they want me, they can come and get me.

Fortunately, I didn't talk to anyone about it. Imagine if I had said to the girls that I was going to do an interview and all that, and then it turned out that Hamid had just taken one too many drags on his playboy friend's joint?

I almost told Halima, who's still squatting with me. And speaking of, I found out how she ended up here. I told you it was just a matter of time.

The other day, I returned to the house with my daughter. It was a Monday night and we were coming back from the baths. I remember it clearly. Halima hadn't heard me in the hallway.

Well, that doesn't surprise me with all the noise around here. The neighbors, the water, the dog in the building opposite who never stops growling. With all that racket, you can't even hear your own thoughts.

Not to mention the wife of the caretaker of the building opposite that opens onto Avenue Hassan II. She missed her true calling. She should have been a muezzin, her voice is so loud. They fight so much, she and her husband, that in the neighborhood, we follow their drama the same way we followed Guadalupe when that soap had just aired.

She can't stand for her stepsister to come visit anymore. He's looking for his blue pants and finds them still hanging out to dry. She goes to her mother's, he goes looking for her. It never ends.

That night, Rabia was also speaking on the telephone with her sister who's married and lives in Italy, and every time, she yells because she can't hear clearly. She says the signal is bad.

If you want my opinion, I don't think the signal has anything to do with it, even if it is shitty. Rabia is deaf and she's the only one who doesn't realize it, that's the truth.

Anyway, back to the story. When Samia and I walked through the door, Halima jumped and I thought I saw her hide something under the cushion beneath her. I'm not in the habit of keeping quiet when something isn't right. Also, she's in my home, so I have a right to know what's going on, don't I?

"What did you hide back there?" I asked her, eyeing the cushion.

My immediate thought was that she had taken something from my cabinet.

"Nothing. I'm watching television."

*Men Dar Lдar** was on the screen. That big hit series about servants, hypocrisy, and poverty. I don't like it. I like the Mexican soaps or the Turkish ones or even the Brazilian ones. I watch the Moroccan series, like everyone, but they aren't my favorite.

Halima adores them. And since I know that she follows all the episodes of the lives of those poor people with great interest, I doubted myself and admitted that maybe my eyes had deceived me. "Maybe she really was just watching TV?" I thought. But the suspicion persisted and since her expression was a little too innocent, I pushed her butt with my hands and I searched beneath the cushion below her.

There, I found a photo of her with two boys. They were seated in a living room with violet tapestries and a big mirror behind them and they were laughing. The two boys were wearing the same outfit. Black pants and a red checkered shirt. They looked about the same age, that of my daughter. When I saw the photo, I looked up at her.

"These are your sons?"

"Yes," she sighed. "Twins."

And her chest rose noisily, in a big puff of air.

"And that's your home?" I added.

I had noticed that she liked the color violet but I didn't expect it to be spread over her entire living room. She doesn't have very good taste, anyway. It shows just by the colors of her djellabas. Sea green and mauve. Does she call those colors? She never wears patterns. And you can see her hair! It's in such a state! She never takes care of it. Not even at the baths. She doesn't use ghassoul* or henna, nothing.

"Yes," she sighed again.

And suddenly, she started to cry, cry, cry. Like an overflowing river. I had never seen such a thing. Even when my father died, no one cried like that. It's not like me to be at a loss for words, but this was too much. I sat down and remained at her side to see if it would end on its own or not.

"Go fetch her some water instead of staring at her like that," I said to my daughter.

She took off running for the kitchenette, the poor thing. From where I was, I saw her take the five-liter canister and pour water into a glass. Since the canister was heavy for her, her arms were shaking. Even so, she didn't spill a single drop on the floor.

"I called home today, and I reached my son," said Halima, sobbing. "I hardly had the time to be happy to hear from him when he recognized my voice and hung up."

"He won't talk to you anymore?" I asked.

She shook her head left to right to say no. Her hair spilled out of her headscarf and her nose was red and swollen. She squeezed her hands together and her fingers were so tense that there was no blood flowing in them anymore. They were somewhere between white and blue.

"It's been more than two years since I've spoken to them. Their father forbids it. And he," indicating the one on the left, "doesn't want anything to do with me."

And she breathed a "thank you," taking the glass of water that my daughter handed to her before sitting on the mattress beneath the window.

From where she was, Samia could see the TV screen; a semsara* had just brought a new servant to the home of a worthless bourgeois woman. Halima was still crying. I said nothing. And just as she had started to cry, in an unending surge, that's how she started to talk.

"Before, I had a husband, kids, a job, a normal life. I was working for a company and I liked my job. I spent a lot of time there. During my lunch break, I would log onto the Internet to chat with my friends. One day, I received a message from someone I didn't know. A man. He told me that he'd noticed me leaving work and had inquired about me. He learned that I managed the customer orders and he called the operator to get my email. He drowned me in compliments, day after day. At first, I didn't respond, but he was so persistent that I started to write him back.

"It lasted the entire summer, and by the end, my heart would race when I noticed one of his emails. From time to time, I said to myself that I shouldn't behave like this, that I was married. I even decided to stop speaking to him, but he sent me photos of flowers and videos of Amr Diab,* because he knew that I liked those things. So I responded to him and it started back up again.

"If I had known ... The more time passed the less I could be without him. He told me his name was Taoufik. When we wrote, he asked me to describe what I was doing, what I was wearing, how I was dressed ... We hadn't met in person yet.

"One day, he gave me a time for us to see each other on the Internet. It was on a Saturday, when my husband was taking the kids out to play soccer. That day, I logged on and we started to talk. I turned on my camera. He told me his had an issue, that it wasn't working that day. He told me I was magnificent and one thing led to another, we became intimate."

All I could see of Halima's face were tears, Kleenex, and the end of her running nose. As she spoke, I pushed tissues in her direction. Her story was interesting but not interesting enough for me to watch her drip snot onto my cushions without doing anything about it. And so that I could concentrate, I ⋅ asked Samia—who had abandoned the TV a while ago and was now listening with her mouth agape— to go buy some bread at the store.

———

"At one point, and I don't know how it happened, I did things that were a bit risqué. I won't give you the details. It happened two weeks in a row. I waited for Saturday impatiently. I hadn't seen him yet. When I asked him to set up his camera, he told me that his looks were nothing compared to mine. He knew how to speak in such a way that he could have made you believe he was speaking to you from paradise, God forgive me."

Halima had stopped crying. Because I know what men are capable of, I understood completely what she was saying.

"The following Monday, I arrived at work and I walked past my boss to say hello. He was in his office and he seemed to be looking at something funny on his screen. When I turned on my computer, I immediately opened my mailbox to read Taoufik's messages. My stomach dropped. It was as if someone had plunged their hand inside of me and ripped my heart out. In several emails were screenshots of me posing for him, messages I had written him, everything...the inside of my body was a giant seesaw. And I didn't know how to stop the motion.

"I didn't dare open my email again until between noon and two o'clock, when the office was empty. Taoufik had sent those messages to everyone: me, my colleagues, my boss, who had been laughing that morning, my husband...everyone.

"I got up, I took my bag and I left. I saw nothing, I heard nothing. But my blood had frozen, and it was burning my skin from the inside. I wandered through the city the entire day, clutching my bag under my arm. If I hadn't feared God, I would have killed myself that day.

"When night fell, I went home. My husband was already there. Seated on a chair in front of the door. The children were seated behind him in the living room. The blood had left their faces, and their lifeless arms were hanging at their sides. I don't have the words to describe that night. Until dawn, the children watched, crying. Every time one of them wanted to protect me, their father sent them flying against the living room wall.

"I was so ashamed that I said nothing as he hit me. Never before that day had I realized that what I was doing from behind the screen was real.

"I'll tell you something: my reflexes made me hide my face, but in reality I was relieved that he hit me. I wanted it to last until I expiated my sins and emerged a virgin again from that affair. Or until I died."

Halima was no longer looking at me. She was no longer there. She recounted the rest in a state of calm.

"After that night, my husband asked for a divorce. The judgment was pronounced very quickly. I didn't try to defend myself. I didn't hire a lawyer. They condemned me to two years in prison for pornography. The last time I saw my husband was the day he brought me the papers from the bank and the notary for something concerning our apartment. I signed them without reading them.

"Since the sentencing, I have been so ashamed that I haven't seen anyone again except one colleague, Nisrine, with whom I was friends at the office. She came to see me once in prison. She told me something that I would have preferred never to know."

Halima slowly shook her head from right to left, her gaze in the void, smiling. She reminded me of a nutjob I'd seen in a film on 2M who was standing in front of a precipice. Before throwing herself off, she'd had exactly the same smile as Halima in that moment.

"She told me that after I left, all anyone could talk about were those photos and my trial. She came thinking that what she would tell me would give me some relief. During the trial, people started gossiping and one day at the office, Wafaa—a secretary I didn't get along with—bragged that she had succeeded in taking me down. Nisrine didn't know all the details, but Taoufik was a distant cousin of Wafaa's.

"They had come up with the plan together. It was simple for them. I didn't even know schemes like that existed. In the moment, I felt betrayed and I wanted to throw up. But now, I don't feel anything anymore. I wait for time to pass and try to stay close to God. You must think that I pray for Him to forgive me. No, I pray for Him to accept my sins as an offering. All my life, God spared me. When my parents died, He gave me an aunt who raised me as her daughter. He gave me a husband, children, a job, health. I took it all for granted.

"I prayed like everyone else but without conviction, and this veil, I only wore it because I didn't want for my husband to be jealous. God did everything for me and I disregarded Him. Today, I am His. And I agreed to go along with the woman who put me in contact with Houcine when I got out of prison because this is what I deserve. God knows that I suffer by doing this. He knows that it's the worst thing that could have happened to me, and I hope that He is happy. Because—for what I did to my children and my husband—hell will not be punishment enough."

Suddenly, like a faucet controlled by an invisible hand, Halima stopped.

At the time, I didn't know what to think. I'd be lying if I told you that her story didn't touch me. And it was when I saw the photo of her children in the living room that I decided to leave my daughter with Mouy.*

Now, she is on vacation at her house in Berrechid. And I don't know yet how I'm going to get her to agree to keep watching her. But with a good amount of money each month, I think I'll manage to convince her. And besides, all women—whores or not—who are in a shitty situation and have parents to lean on leave their children with their mothers, so why shouldn't I?

Anyway, in that moment, I felt sorry for Halima, but now that I've had time to really reflect, I think she has only herself to blame.

Her main problem is that she's not a capable woman.

We found ourselves here not because we didn't have a choice. Not because we did childish things behind a screen and then we didn't know how to defend ourselves. Before she came here, she was in prison. And before prison, she was married and had a home. How many people do you know like that? How many people do you know who are so incompetent that they suffer a single, fatal fall? Without so much as a stumble beforehand?

I say that if it happens to you, it's because you're not looking in front of you and you're moving forward like a donkey. And the day when you seek the person responsible, you can't blame anyone but yourself.

WEDNESDAY THE 21ST

I'm on the bus to Berrechid. I still haven't heard anything from Hamid. I tried to call him, but once again, that moron didn't pick up. His loss. Because today, I'm leaving the city for a month.

I'm seated by the window, the road goes by outside. At this time of year, everything is yellow. And the fields are all razed. This year, the harvests were meager, they said. But you shouldn't pay attention to them. They say that every year to inflate their prices.

A woman as big as an oil drum is sitting to my left and her children—two rather tall boys—are in the two seats in the next row. I'll be okay during the trip because she knows how to contain them. The shouts of children have always bothered me. And today I'm more likely to be set off than other days. I stop drinking when I go to Mouy's. And even with the pills I down to knock myself out, it doesn't take much for me to blow a fuse.

When they all got on the bus, her sons were bickering behind her. When she asked me as she sat down if she could take the seat, the two brats were fighting. She couldn't see them because she bent down to place her bag beneath the seat in front of her. But she didn't need to have eyes on the back of her head to realize they were acting foolish. As she stood up, she flung her hand at one son's cheek and as she turned around, it struck the other's back.

I laughed, thinking, "Now that's skill." But I laughed in my head, not out loud.

"Shut up, you asses!" she yelled.

And she turned toward me, saying, "These kids are going to drive me insane."

"God rewards parents for their sacrifices," I responded mechanically, adjusting myself on my seat to make room for her.

It's stiflingly hot, and the bus station was swarming with people. Fortunately I have muscular arms. When I saw all those people, I put my hands in the pockets of my djellaba, I stuck out my elbows and *anafa*! That's what you have to do with these people. Elbows and clubs are the only things that work. If I hadn't done that, I'd still be over there getting a tan at this hour.

On top of it, since it's Ramadan in a few days, everyone is on the move, everyone is taking a trip, everyone is going somewhere. And you should see what they lug around with them. I've brought hardly anything. When I travel, I bring the bare minimum. I put the mkharka* that I bought from Rkia in a big bag with dates, and my clothes in a shopping bag. Mouy will like Rkia's mkharka. It's exceptional.

I asked her to prepare it for me a month ago. She does it in her home at Derb Sultan and everyone fights to have some. Since I've known her for several years, she doesn't even argue when I place my order, even if she has to put her sister's on hold to fulfill it. And at a good price too. Thirty-five dirhams per kilo. I've brought enough to last the entire month.

Every year, I spend Ramadan with my mother. Work or not, I have no interest in missing Ramadan with Mouy. Even though it's a month when the girls get good work in the neighborhood, I take off.

It's always been like that, even when I had a home of my own. And the truth is that it's a break for me too. Even if Mouy doesn't leave you a moment of rest. When I'm at the house with her, she doesn't let me watch TV in peace. Go do this, go do that. She loves chores. As soon as she sees something that's not shiny, she gets up. Sometimes, I get tired just watching her.

Physically, I'm a lot like her. She was very beautiful in her youth, like I was. Tall, strong, curvy, thick hair down to the knees, straight and black. Still today, she has to coil her hair a good dozen times to gather it into a bun on her head.

And she is strong. You should have seen her when she was younger! Her hands could knead dough all day long without getting tired. She didn't need my father to slit the throats of the chicken or the sheep. God rest his soul, he never argued with Mouy. Even if he was also tough and could have broken her front teeth with half a punch if he wanted.

In any event, he didn't spend much time in the house.

Until he fell ill and became bedridden, Ba was never at home. He was a hard worker. When we were still in the countryside, he spent the day outdoors. When he wasn't working, he was stacking hay. When he wasn't planting, he was uprooting something or other.

And when we moved into town—I must have been about fifteen years old—he didn't come back home until late at night. Mouy served him dinner, and he would sleep until the next day. He would work at the souk, in the grain barn.

And one day, he fell ill. I couldn't tell you what it was exactly, some kind of bacteria started to eat away at him from the inside.

And from then on, there was nothing left of him. He became as skinny as my little finger. The poor man grew so weak that he could no longer speak, no longer eat. We brought him to the doctor but he said there was nothing to do for him.

So we brought him back to the house, where he spent the day sitting in the corner of the two mattresses in the living room awaiting his death in front of the TV. I don't think he could see the screen anymore. It's possible he couldn't tell the difference between the images and the zellige* Mouy used to cover the walls. A beautiful zellige, blue with orange, green, and white.

One night, we had just finished dinner. My brothers had gone out to smoke their cigarettes in the street, and Mouy, the wives of my brothers, and I were cleaning up. Ba was in his usual spot. When we were done cleaning, Farida, the wife of my youngest brother, prepared tea and we sat down to talk and joke around a bit.

At one point, Mouy said to me, "Help your father, I think he wants to turn around."

Since he had moved, the covers had slid down his shoulder. And when I leaned toward him to help, he was gone. It was as simple as that. No sound, no hospital. Nothing. You're at home, you hear your loved ones speaking around you, and you close your eyes. Forever. Is there anyone luckier than him?

Mouy still lives in that house. In the beginning, when they built it, we lived on the second floor. But as soon as she started having her knee problems, she could no longer climb the stairs. So instead of shedding some pounds by following a diet as the doctor had advised, she chose to move down a floor. She said that she hadn't spent her entire life maintaining her curves for some charlatan to send her back to square one with a green salad. Mouy is stubborn.

"You want some?" says the oil drum to my left, handing me a bimo.*

I take the cookie even though I don't want it. You don't say no in these situations.

"Where are you going?" she asks, arranging her green djellaba around her shoulders.

"To Berrechid, to my mother's house. And you?"

I'm sweating and I wipe the beads of perspiration pearling at my forehead every minute. She is also sweating, but it doesn't stop her from talking.

"To Marrakech. Do you live in Casa?" she asks me.

"Yes, I take care of my poor sick aunt," I tell her, offering her a bit of water from the bottle I filled at the house.

The sick aunt who exists only in your imagination is very useful in cases like this, when you meet someone you don't know but whom you'd like to talk with.

Everyone has a sick aunt, don't they? Or a dying one. Or something along those lines. But you can't use this story with the people close to you. With them, you need a more elaborate version. With Mouy, for example, I have another story.

As soon as my husband left, I told her that I was staying in Casablanca to clean houses. Not that I was a lowly maid, no. Mouy would never have tolerated the idea that her daughter was scrubbing people's grime while being treated like a slave. As far as Mouy knows, I do proper cleaning. No mopping, no sweeping. I have a machine, I sit on top of it, and that's how it's done. A company job. I saw it in a movie.

And I told her that on the side—for some extra cash—I sell contraband, with products brought to me from the North that I resell here. That's what I told her. And it worked. So I don't have too many problems with her. The thing that really causes issues for me is that every time I go to see her, she grills me about what's going on with my bastard of a husband. And each time, she's more insistent than the last.

Well, he and I—his name is Hamid too—we're no longer married but our story isn't over yet. I'll tell you about it one day.

I'm at Berrechid.

On the way here, my neighbor told me her entire life story. Her mother, her father, her sisters, her husband, her children, what she likes to eat for iftar,* the cakes she eats to break the fast for Eid.

Everything. Even without cigarettes, the journey passed quickly.

I've just arrived in our neighborhood. The taxi dropped me off on the avenue and now I'm walking home. The houses, the businesses, everything is exactly how I left it. The mosque is still in its place. The power station too. There's maybe a bit more graffiti on those gray walls over there.

The pepita seller is still opposite the laundromat. And Brahim, the neighbor's son, is leaning against the wall. Each time I see him, he's in that same pose: balanced on one leg, a joint in his hand. Sometimes he's on his left leg, sometimes on his right. That's the only thing that ever changes.

Children are playing soccer in the street. Three or four surround Brahim. They ask him to tell them jokes. They always do that. He tells jokes or he doesn't depending on his mood. And on the quality of what he has in his hand. Sometimes he laughs, and sometimes he remains standing like a stork in its nest.

I'm at our house. It's like all the others. We have a ground floor where there's a garage that my mother rents to a guy who operates a call shop out of it. And the front door, red iron, opens onto a staircase that leads to the upper floors. There are three. Not including the roof, where we slaughter the sheep for Eid. My brothers and their wives live above Mouy. Abdelhak on the second floor, Abdelilah on the third floor. Nothing's changed here either. The red door is still red. And the key on the ledge is still in its place too. I spend a moment looking for it, my fingers run from right to left. I climb the stairs and already I can hear my mother talking. She's telling my brothers' wives which cakes they have to prepare for Ramadan.

"Okay, so we all know the plan, you, you go buy what we need to make the cakes. And don't forget to buy a baking sheet. Ours sticks."

As usual, she's the boss.

"I've got the mkharka," I say, entering the living room, where they're seated around the table, and lifting my bag to indicate that the cakes are inside.

All three turn toward the door where I'm standing. My mother is in the exact place where my father passed away. In front of them is a tray with tea, bread, and olive oil. I put down my bag and take off my sandals without bending down.

Mouy is half lying on her side and when she sees me, she straightens up a bit, just enough to extend her hand for me to kiss on both sides. The back then the palm. No matter what they say, a mother's hand is sacred. I squeeze it tight against me after having kissed the front.

Samia jumps on me. She's grown since the last time I saw her. And she's become more beautiful. Mouy might be difficult but what's undeniable is that she takes good care of my daughter.

I greet my brothers' wives. They fuss over my cheeks several times, making noise and kissing the void. I don't like them very much. Neither of them, each for her own reasons. One of them is always looking to start a fight with me.

And what bothers me about it is that they go through my brothers, who then speak to my mother, who then comes to tell me what they said. Why don't they speak to me directly? I don't like those games. And if they're too afraid, then they can shut their mouths.

"How was the trip?"

"It was good, Mouy, good."

Her eyes scan me.

"It wasn't too hot?"

"It was, hot as hell."

She pours tea and, eyeing my toes for some unknown reason, says, "Was finding transport to get here easy?"

"Yes, Mouy, thank you."

And she hands me the glass, scrutinizes my ears, "And work, how is it? Everything's going well?"

She doesn't leave a second of pause between my responses and the next question. I can feel her interrogation coming. In another question or two, there'll be the one I don't want to hear, especially not in front of those two. Afterward, they'll brag about their men and their children and their house. As if they were better than me.

"That damn idiot hasn't shown any sign of life?"

What did I tell you?

"That damn idiot," as she calls him—believe it or not—is my husband. It's a long story, and even though I don't really want to get into it, it's time for me to tell you.

I met Hamid two or three years after we settled in Berrechid. I must have been seventeen or eighteen years old. The first time I saw him, he was on his motorcycle, a Peugeot 103 that backfired all over the neighborhood. He was a friend of my brothers. They called him the tailor because he spent his days weaving between the streets with his motorcycle like a tailor with his needle between fabrics.

The first thing I noticed about him was his hair. It was the end of a summer day, long as death. The sun was still beating strong. Beneath its reflection, Hamid's hair was shining like the tailpipe of his motorcycle. He had tons of hair, black as nigella seed. People say that nigella protects from the evil eye. I can't tell you whether that's true or not. But I can tell you that it certainly pierced my eyes.

Since things were going pretty well for him, he was always well dressed. He was tall and thin but strong. An Arab beauty, with thick eyebrows. I was crazy about him. All the girls in the neighborhood were.

From time to time, I passed him as I was going to buy something at the bakery, and he would ask me to call one of my brothers if he was at the house. At that time, my four brothers still lived with our parents. Abdelilah, Abdelhak, Abdelaziz, and Abdelkrim.

Over time, he started to talk to me and smile at me. I liked him so much my heart would beat out of my chest every time he looked at me. You know how it is when you're young. One look sets you ablaze.

We started talking to each other. And over time, we went from "let's talk" to "let's kiss" and then to "let's touch." And after that we wanted to do other things.

Since I took a little too long each time I went to the bakery, Mouy—who was starting to suspect something—tightened the screws. And one day, she caught me red-handed. We were kissing between two walls. He had his hand pressed against one of my breasts. My breast was so big that it was popping out from between his fingers.

No need to tell you the beating I got that day. It was the worst beating I'd ever received, second only to the one about two weeks later. Since I couldn't go out anymore, I spent the day going up and down from the roof to lay out the laundry or to check whether it was dry. That's how we saw each other until my mother caught us once again.

When she reached the roof, he took off, and Mouy called my brothers to tell them to go tell that damned guy, that bastard, that swine, that hooligan, and countless other names not to prowl around here anymore unless he was looking for someone to shave his head. And then, she took care of me. I cried and screamed. If I had known where all of it would lead, I would have gone to a hammam to ease my tension and then gone and relaxed beneath the covers. But I was too young for that and it was still eating away at me down there.

The days passed, and I continued to cry and act as if I were in a movie. I refused to eat, I refused to bathe. Neither Mouy's beatings nor Ba's could do anything to combat it. Mouy was going insane, at a loss for what to do with me. One day, without warning, while we were eating, she turned toward me and said in front of everyone, "The only solution for you is marriage."

She said to my older brother, pointing her finger at him, "Are you the one who knows him the best? Or is it you?" turning toward another of my brothers.

Without waiting for a response, she added, looking between the two of them so that the one who felt the most targeted would act: "You'll go see the kid and you'll tell him to bring his mother here so I can talk to her. And you, I'm warning you," she said to me, pointing her right index finger at me and her opposite eyebrow toward the sky, "don't come cry-ing to me the day when things go south with him."

I learned much later that Mouy expected Hamid to take off when he heard wind of serious talk. But that's not what happened.

In the end, his mother came. She brought sug-arloaves, tea, and her two daughters, in case my mother wanted one of them for her sons.

My mother had loaned me one of her light beige outfits, simple, without a belt. And she had braided my hair. I served the tea. I had prepared msemens* and butter cakes. They sat down and they spoke.

Not long after, we were married. I don't think I've ever been so happy in my life. All the more so because I had snatched him away from the other girls.

We had a beautiful celebration. We slaughtered a sheep, the family came, the neighbors came. The family of the groom sent a cow! Big, hefty, black and white. I saw it arrive from a distance through the window of the bedroom where they had put me to get ready. It took up the entire street. And you should have seen how they decorated its forehead: they had made it the most beautiful mint crown I had ever seen. It was really something. It was so beautiful that I let out the biggest youyou of my life. It lasted such a long time that as I was still letting loose, Mouy had the time to come down from the roof where she was doing who knows what, come up behind me, take off her sandal and throw it at the back of my head yelling that a bride doesn't yell her own youyous, that it was a jinx and that today, since she was going to be rid of me, was an important day.

At my wedding, the women danced and the guests ate well. We had the best couscous! If the plates could talk, you wouldn't have been able to distinguish their youyous from those of the women. My mother certainly knows how to make couscous. And I do too. When a pregnant woman has a craving, it's always my couscous they ask for. When I was born, my mother rubbed a chicken liver in my palms so that I would know how to cook. And I can make rfissate*! You'd gobble up your fingers along with it.

The other day, I was with the girls and I served them a couscous with meat and vegetables. There was squash, zucchini, turnips, carrots, eggplants, onions; all God's vegetables were in it. As we ate, Samira said, "Jmiaa, if you cooked for weddings, you would be as famous as Choumicha.*"

And the jealous Jahar said to her, "You mean Bargache*?" implying that I'm fat.

"All the women who can remember Bargache are taking care of their grandchildren at this hour," Samira snapped back.

We had a good laugh.

After the celebration of my wedding, we stayed in Berrechid for a little while at my mother's house, and then Hamid suggested that we go live in Casa. There's work over there, he said.

We left. We rented a bedroom in the home of an elderly woman we called Lhajja.*

In the beginning, Hamid went out in the morning to go to work. I don't know what he did exactly, but the important thing is that he brought back money.

I spent the day at the house, either watching the television or listening to music—Najat Aatabou* most of the time. Hamid had given me a cassette of her music when we were still in Berrechid, and since that time, Najat had become like a sister to me. I know all her songs by heart, and I've never missed one of her performances on television.

At the time, I listened to her songs without much thought, but now I know what I like about her: it's that she always sings about ordinary things, seemingly banal stories that could happen to anyone a thousand times a day. There's always a moment in her songs when she says something that's exactly what happened to you. As if she were with you at that moment. Or as if her brain were connected to yours when she sat down to write. She kept me good company.

And when Hamid returned at the end of the day, we would have a snack and spend the night together. It was wonderful. And since there's nothing better than the truth, the truth is that every day, I was like a bride on her wedding night. He would come back and he would find me lying down, propped on my side on one elbow, a hand placed on my plump thighs, watching the television. Scheherazade on her honeymoon bed! As if I had spent the day posing like a whore in front of the television.

As soon as he opened the door and saw me like that, he would jump right on top of me. He would forget about the joint he had planned to smoke, about his friends he would sometimes grab coffee with, and everything else. It all faded away, and the only thing he saw was a human-sized cake filled with cream, posed on his bed like a gift from God.

On Sundays we would usually go for a walk. We would go to the square with the pigeons, next to the fountain. I would put on my wedding djellaba—green, with golden embroidery on the front, the side, and the sleeves. We would walk down Avenue Hassan II and eat pepitas. We would stop to eat snails. All the women would stare at us, we were so beautiful. We laughed a lot together, I don't remember what about. It would be like that through our entire walk. He would laugh and I would laugh. As if our laughs were speaking to each other.

When we went on walks and I held him by the arm, his chest would inflate like a peacock deploying its tail. It was like what you see in movies. The hero is beautiful, well dressed, well mannered. And the girl who's with him is smiling, joyous. You don't even need to hear what they're saying to understand what's happening. There's just background music.

But where do movies get it from, do you know? They get it from real life. The problem is that those sons of bitches who write the stories, they don't tell you where it leads in the end. No, they know to stop the story after the wedding day. When your stomach is still bloated and you smile so much that your teeth are about to fall out and start wriggling around with the guests. What comes after isn't their problem. Because if they tell you what comes next, you won't go see their shitty movie.

And then, the two worthless months of the honeymoon phase passed. And little by little, things started to change. In the moment, I didn't realize. It began insidiously, like an illness. By the time I understood, they had already rolled me in a shroud.

Hamid started to leave the house later and later in the morning. He had taken a job with a real estate agent: he found clients to buy and sell houses and he was given commissions on the sales. Just like Chaïba's Belaïd or Saïd. From time to time, he also sold cars. That's what he told me. And that's how he justified coming home sometimes with a fat stack of money, and other times bringing back nothing. The irregular income didn't bother me. When he gave me more than I needed, I hid the extra in the closet with my things. And so he wouldn't realize I was setting money aside, I kept asking him for money every Friday. But when he didn't have any, I didn't insist.

Hamid would get angry very quickly. When I felt it happening, I didn't leave him the time to pick a fight with me. I quickly found something else to do. Like go fetch the oil I had forgotten at the store. Or the Laughing Cow. Or a tin of sardines. Or whatever would make me disappear from his sight.

But sometimes, he cornered me before I could leave. When that happened, I knew I was done for.

What you need to know to understand what I'm saying is that Hamid loved his joints. And that there's nothing worse than joints, even if everyone smokes them—from kids to the elderly—and even if they say that it grows out of the sidewalks it's so common. I've seen the darkest oddities in my life but I've never seen a sickness like hashish.

Hashish is a sweet sickness. It enters gently into the skin, it's cool, cheerful. It makes you feel good. You want to be in its arms, you want it to cradle you like your mother did. It has the same effect each time, it reassures you. And your friends who smoke, they're also cool and nice. And you're all in the arms of the same mother. You're all brothers. And you love each other. And then one day, you don't know why, like a cat, the mother takes one of her little ones and eats it. Just like that. Why that one? Why not his brother? God only knows. The others who are with you, they continue to puff on their joints, they don't move. They watch it gobble you up, hovering between the soporific effect and the fear that the same thing will happen to them.

But to understand that, you have to live it. Since I wasn't familiar with it, I let Hamid smoke as much as he wanted. The problem is that cat with her little ones. Of all the litter, she chose Hamid. He became paranoid. He suspected everything he saw or heard.

Hamid wore me out when he smoked. He would spend hours talking into the void. It started with something trivial and then we would inevitably dig up things from the past, like that night when we were sitting peacefully at the house. He was going out to meet his friends, and I was watching an Egyptian show.

"Where are my black pants?" he asked me, his head in the closet, his arm going back and forth between the armoire and the bed, throwing clothes around.

"Ask before you gut the entire armoire. I washed them, they're on the roof drying," I responded, pushing away the clothes that had ended up next to me, without taking my eyes off the television.

After a moment of silence: "Why do you watch this shitty show?" he said to me with a grimace crumpling his face, his head turned toward the screen. "Gamel Pacha spends his day greasing his hair for his whore secretary, and you, do you see yourself in Amel?" he added.

On the screen, Nawel, or whatever her name was, was flaunting herself in her boss's office, so that he would ditch his wife and take her on a cruise down the Nile. It was long before Mexican soaps were available on our TVs.

"Her name's not Amel," I said to avoid answering the question.

"Okay, her name's not Amel, but his name is Gamel Pacha, right?" he answered, wriggling around to imitate the image he had of the hunk.

"What do you care?" And I added, getting up, "Hang on, I'm going up to see if your pants are dry."

"You are not going up or down. You will sit here and you will speak to me," he said, pointing at the bed.

And then we were off. As soon as he got me to sit down, I was done for. The sparring began. Question after question. I defended myself. Don't think that I just let it happen. That's not my way. But the difference between him and me is that he didn't feel exhaustion. He never got short of breath when he argued. I wasn't used to it yet.

I remember very clearly the sensation that I felt during those never-ending fights. When he started to grill me, it was like he inserted a worm into my stomach. And that worm was eating whatever it found there, very slowly. It grew bigger, grew bigger, grew bigger until it replaced my intestines, climbed up my throat and reached my brain. Once there, the first thing the worm did was block my ears. It ate the canal that led to the orifices, and my ears plugged up. I couldn't hear anything anymore. It made me want to hurl. And then, it attacked my brain. I wanted to sever my head from my neck, set it on the table and leave. I wanted for all of it to be over. While this happened, Hamid continued to move his lips at me, asking question after question. Eventually, I don't know why, he would stop talking and leave. He would stop at the point when I was emptied, when I felt hollow as a jug. As if he and the worm were one and the same. And he knew that there was nothing left to eat.

On top of the paranoia, the joints, his anxiety, and the money that was becoming increasingly rare, he added alcohol. When I first met him, he would drink Saturday nights with his friends. For a bit of fun. When we arrived in Casa, and since he no longer had his mother watching over him, he started to drink a little more.

He would go out and drink with his friends at the end of the day before coming home for dinner.

From time to time, he would go out again after dinner too. And then it started to happen more frequently. On the one hand, it suited me because he was starting to wear me out. But on the other, it got under my skin because I didn't like the idea that he was tired of me. That's what happens when you marry someone you love: sooner or later, he abandons you. And all that remains are the cold cinders from the blaze you thought could roast lambs by the thousands.

He stopped coming home at night to eat with me. The first few times, I waited for him while falling asleep in front of the television, but he would show up late, and he reeked. A stench of cigarettes and wine that turned my stomach. I hated it. Especially because he liked to climb on top of me in that state. As I was sleeping, I felt him enter and hump me, rigid like a donkey in heat. My nose detected him before my thighs. And then over time, I stopped wanting to touch him, even when he was sober.

Sometimes, at night, he wouldn't even be able to make it to our bed. And more and more regularly, he would puke his guts out onto the floor. The next day, I would clean everything. His vomit on the floor and my soiled sheets. Even then, I didn't say a thing. I let him do it, telling myself that it would pass, that he was still young and he would settle down like everyone else. But it became the norm, and the more time passed the more sick of it I got. I would get up in the morning, my mood like disheveled hair, and shout at Hamid, who was only half listening from within his fog. And then I would shut up so the neighbors didn't hear us. I would never have been able to bear the thought that they knew what was going on in our home.

One day, I realized that Hamid was no longer bothering to get up for work. God only knows how he was bringing money home. He would get up in the middle of the afternoon, he would have his coffee with milk while smoking a cigarette, and he would go to the café to find his friends. That was his work. Go to the café and dream up plans that would score him loads of cash.

Sell contraband merchandise brought back from the North, gas from the South, open a dairy with his sister... Each day brought its share of ideas that would enrich him. One day, he came home with what he called the best opportunity he'd ever had in his life: one of his friends had proposed that he invest ten thousand dirhams in merchandise from China. Bundles filled with glasses, sandals, sheets. He planned to buy the merchandise and sell it off at Derb Omar.* He said he would start out that way, buy another lot of merchandise, and continue on like that until he became rich.

He borrowed the money from his mother. God only knows what she sold to help him out. The day when he came back from Berrechid with the money, he went out with his friend to celebrate their incredible future business partnership. It was a party, and what a party! He went out with ten thousand dirhams, he came back with nothing. He didn't even realize it until he woke up the next morning. The money had flown away. He had hidden it in the inside pocket of his jacket, he said! Was he out of his mind?

He spent the day searching for the money. Outside first, then in the house. He emptied the contents of our armoire onto the bed and the floor. He rifled through all my things. He even tore out the inside pocket of his jacket to make sure the bills hadn't slid into the lining. When he realized that all trace of his money had disappeared, that's when he turned his sights on me.

To help him, like an idiot, I asked him to retrace his steps from the night before, telling him to try to remember where he had been exactly, the places he might have forgotten. By way of response and telling me to mind my own business, he slapped me so hard he gave me a black eye. It was the first time he had raised a hand to me. And from that day on, his hand would remain high, searching for any pretext to land on my face.

When it was out of jealousy, I said nothing because I understood, but when it was because he just needed to cool off, then I would fly off the handle and I would hit him too, I'd smack him right in the face.

I couldn't tell you where that money went. In any event, the story ended with him kissing my feet and hands so that I would give him my bracelets and the gold chain he had gifted me on our wedding day. By the time I had given in and he'd sold them along with his motorcycle, it was too late for him to buy the merchandise. The container from China had left the port.

So he gave the money from my gold to his mother and he was back at square one.

That was when he lost it. He couldn't bear being duped. The day he had planned to return the money to his mother, he gave her a magnificent scarf telling her that thanks to her, he had managed to get his business going. And that he would start to earn a decent amount of money and would be able to pay her back for all the good she had done for him.

In the end, he exaggerated the story so much that it was as if he'd started believing it. And the two pennies he managed to earn were no longer enough. Now he thought only of money and how to get his hands on it. But even so, don't imagine that he tried for even a minute to sort out a real job. To get work, having a tongue that tells tall tales is not enough. No, to get work, you need a good head on your shoulders. And Hamid only had the outline.

I think I still loved him. Or else, since I was still a bit of an idiot, I thought it might pass. I had hope.

Despite our arguments and our brawls, I still forgave him. How did we arrive at what came next, at such a loss? I can't tell you. We advanced along our path until we found ourselves here, and that's that.

*O*ne night, we were at the house, about to eat dinner: Hamid, a friend of his, and me. He often brought friends to the house. I made them food, they drank one or two bottles of wine, and they went to the bar. We usually fought when he got back. I said nothing about the cigarettes, nothing about the hashish, nothing about the alcohol, but it pissed me off when he brought his friends over. I felt unwanted when they were there.

That night, I had prepared a tagine with potatoes and tomatoes. He and his friend were sitting on the mattress, and they were passing the white plastic cup they were using as an ashtray back and forth, smoking cigarettes and waiting for me to serve them dinner. They were listening to chikhate* on the VCR that I'd brought from my parents' house.

After dinner, Hamid got up and left, saying, "I'm going to buy cigarettes and wine at the guerrab.* I won't be long."

I was brooding in the bedroom when I noticed his friend's feet behind me.

"Do you need something?" I asked him, trying to mask my irritation.

I had barely finished my sentence when suddenly I couldn't move. He had jumped on me, clasping his hand in front of my mouth and grabbing me from behind. On one side, I was trapped by the wall; on the other by his leg that he had wrapped around mine. He was pressed up against me and he was rubbing his rod against my ass, trying to lower his pants with his free hand.

I struggled, but he was strong as an ox. I tried to scream. He smothered me. My neck was twisted, and I couldn't move anymore without getting an electric shock. I thought of the neighbors, if they came and saw this spectacle. His hand lifted my dress. I thought of my husband, who would come back and find me in this position. He yanked down my underwear.

I bit him, contorting myself like a worm and calling for Hamid. He squeezed his hand over my mouth even harder and whispered into my ear: "Hamid? Don't tell me he didn't warn you?"

What he said stunned me. It was a sharp blow. I stopped moving until he finished. He pulled his pants back up and went to sit and smoke a cigarette with his orange lighter, his zipper still open. He smoked, taking his time, before getting up to leave. It wasn't until he left that I noticed the bottle and the pack of cigarettes on the table were still full. Hamid had had no reason to go out and buy more.

When Hamid came back, he headed to the armoire, as if nothing had happened. He didn't ask me why his friend was no longer there. He came back empty-handed, and his eyes didn't meet mine.

That night went by in slow motion. Hamid and I fought until morning. He tried to stop the fight but I kept reentering the fray. I didn't let him rest for a second. After, he too was like a madman.

We swung at each other, but our blows were muffled. We smacked against the walls. From time to time, we found ourselves on the bed, trying to catch our breath before getting up once more to really lay into each other. Gritting my teeth, I asked him to tell me why he'd done it. And I cried with rage. And the more the tears flowed the more I detested him. And I detested myself for making a spectacle of myself in front of him. I pictured my mother telling me that he wasn't the man for me, I thought of the other neighborhood girls who hadn't fought for him, who had let me take him, I thought of my insistence on being with him...

After a moment, I had only one idea in my head: for him to be inside me. The grimace of disgust on his face when I told him to do it made my blood boil: "I'm the disgusting one? You gave me to that other piece of shit and I'm the one who's disgusting? Okay, now, you're going to fuck me. You're going to fuck me and you're going to put it where your friend just was."

I was unleashed and I couldn't even breathe, so badly did it hurt when the air entered my lungs. The more he rejected me the more I threw myself at him, shoving my breasts in his face. I grabbed them, I squeezed them. I thrust them under his nose:

"Here, look, this is what your friend did. Yeah, the one who was just here, the one who fucked me."

He tried to pull on my wrists to remove my hands from my breasts. In the moment I felt nothing but I was pressing them so hard that night that the next day, I found the violet trace of my fingers diagonally across my chest.

What did me in, what made me give up the fight, was when, grabbing at his crotch to crush his balls, I felt that he was hard. Despite everything, he had a boner. And that was that. I had no more desire to struggle.

As soon as he felt me drained of my strength, he wanted me. He tore off what remained of my dress and he got on top of me, calling me all kinds of names and ripping out my hair.

I didn't move again until morning.

At dawn, he went out. My arm turned on the television and I stayed sitting in front of it, without moving, watching the film of the previous night play out in my mind. I didn't eat, didn't go to the bathroom, didn't change my clothes.

When he came home to change and go back out again, my stare remained glued to the television. I had turned it off but my eyes didn't move. In the reflection of the screen, I saw him—while changing—drop money out of the pocket of his jacket. My money. A small stack, which he gathered and counted in front of the armoire. He took a two thousand rial note from the four in the stack. He placed it on the table without saying anything to me and he went out. I didn't move, didn't look at him.

When he came back, it was the next day. Or the day after that. Or who knows what day it was? And who cares anyway?

That same day repeated on a loop, blurry like a haze; with the television that went off or on now and then. And the water and bread that my fingers brought to my mouth.

Still today, despite the years that have passed, sometimes I return to that moment in my mind. When that happens, I stay in my bedroom and do nothing.

$\mathcal{T}$he second time it happened was a few days later. He took me by surprise. That son of a bitch didn't leave me the time to realize what was going on. If I'd been able to reflect, emerge from my coma, or if I'd had even half of the capacities that I have now, I would never have let him come near me again.

That night, he had just come home.

"What's for dinner?" he asked.

I didn't respond.

"I'm talking to you, what are we having for dinner?" he repeated in an irritated tone.

"I don't know what we're eating," I said, turning to look at him for the first time since the incident.

"If you don't know what we're eating, who does know then?" he answered, grimacing and turning toward the door, as if to leave again.

Then, suddenly, he turned back toward me, as if he had changed into someone else.

"You know what, let's stop all of this."

He approached me. He reached his arms toward me and he said, "That's enough. Come here."

He was calm.

"Come," he repeated.

He brought me toward him, grabbing me by the forearms. I pushed him away, hitting him.

He said again: "Come."

I scratched him. He continued: "Come."

That back-and-forth lasted for a moment. Then his calm won me over. He brought me to him and I said nothing. His arms were rough but his torso was warm.

"Listen, let's stop all this. All of it, it was nothing."

"..."

"Trust me, it'll pass."

"..."

"I told you, things like that, they happen all the time."

"..."

"You don't know because you don't know anything about life yet. But it's nothing."

"... *(Nothing at all? Trust you?)*"

"Listen, we can get out of the shit we're in."

"... *(It'll pass? And if it had happened to you, would it still pass then too?)*"

"We can make a bunch of money quickly and move on to something else."

"... *(Get out of this shit? Is there worse shit than what you've dragged me into?)*"

"I've come up with the perfect plan. I just need a few things. I don't need much. And you know, I have no one I can count on other than you."

"... *(And from the start, did you talk to me in the street so you could one day do this to me?)*"

"I have no one else I can rely on besides you."

"... *(I have a family, I have brothers, I don't need anyone.)*"

"Anyway, you know, it'll go quickly. I just need a bit of money to buy the merchandise, and then it'll be over."

"... *(I don't need you.)*"

"Listen, I know another guy, Abdenbi, he has contacts in China. You give him an order, he buys the stuff, and he delivers it to you when it arrives…"

"… (And if I wanted to, I would show you and your crappy plans how you make money.)"

"You choose the merchandise yourself…"

"… (You haven't seen what I'm capable of yet.)"

"You don't end up stuck with a bundle of some things that sell and some that don't. From the beginning, you know what you're getting. If I ask you for anything again after this plan, cut off this tongue talking to you."

"… (Cut off this tongue talking to me? You really don't know me at all. It's not your tongue I'm going to cut off.)"

"And you can find buyers before even placing the order. Not all of them, but a portion of them. Or else you can strike up an agreement with the store owners, for them to sell the merchandise in advance."

"… (And now, we do what? You told your mother that you had become a billionaire, and I, I do what? I go to Mouy and tell her everything?)"

"There are plenty in Derb Omar. I'll go to them, we'll partner up, and I'll place the order afterward."

"… (Or else I tell her stories about China?)"

"I've given it a lot of thought and I know it's going to work. I'm thinking I'll buy sandals, buckets, soap dishes, little stools, plastic mats, towels."

"… (First off, you'd be better off keeping that big mouth of yours shut. How do you know what sells and what doesn't sell?)"

"Only utensils for the hammam. Everyone goes to the hammam. Women, men, children. Everyone."

"… (If not for me, you'd still be up shit creek.)"

"There isn't anyone who doesn't go to the bath."

"… (Yes, you've really given it some thought, it's obvious.)"

"Look at me, it's going to work. I just need some money to get started. Afterward, you and I will forget all of this and we'll move on."

"… (And that bad luck that follows you everywhere, have you thought about that bad luck?)"

"I won't be had like the last time. You can't imagine how much that destroyed me, because I don't tell you what's going on inside me. This time, you'll take care of everything. You'll keep the money. And you'll come with me to put it in the importer's hands."

"…"

"Listen, the plan is solid. You don't have to be afraid of anything. And look at me, you're all I have. You know that? Don't you know that?"

"…"

"I'll do everything I can for us to be well-off and for you to live better than you did in your parents' house. This is just a rough patch. I know what I'm doing. I swear to you that this plan will work."

"…"

"Look at me. We'll collect what we need to get going and after we'll do two or three more import operations like these with our capital and we'll start back from zero."

"... *(You're lucky that I'm not one of those sluts. One of those who take you, suck you dry, and then ditch you.)*"

"And then, we'll go back to Berrechid. I thought we could open a café-restaurant. And work there together."

"... *(Suck you dry. Pussies like you, that's what you deserve.)*"

"I didn't tell you but I was there the day before yesterday. I found a place."

"... *(Yes, you need a slut that'll take you and leave you. Like the piece of shit you are.)*"

"I'll take care of the supplies and the cash register."

"... *(Yeah, that's right. You'll man the cash register. The woman who lets you man the cash register is crazy, out of her mind. The woman who lets you man the cash register is an idiot.)*"

"With your cooking skills, you'll blow away the competition. No other restaurant in Berrechid will have any customers left."

"... *(People like you shouldn't be allowed anywhere near a cash register. People like you, all you should have access to is the mop. You won't get past me. Or else, at most, I'll let you serve.)*"

"And we'll be near our families. Your mother will be happy. And proud."

"... *(Did you think you'd be at the cash register posing in front of customers? Dressed in a suit, with your hair slicked back?)*"

"So, what do you say?"

"... *(No one will touch the cash register apart from me. And if you think I'm going to cook for your customers, you're dreaming.)*"

"Are you listening to me?"

"... *(Before the opening, I'll hire girls, my cousins on my father's side, I'll teach them what they need to know in the kitchen, and I'll move on to more serious matters.)*"

"I told you: after, we'll move on to something else. And we'll never speak of this again."

"... *(And you, loser, I promise you, you'll never go anywhere near the money.)*"

"Talk to me, please, don't be like this. Jmiaa..."

"And if you get scammed by the guy you have to pay in advance?"

And that's when it all started. I can't tell you why I said yes. The only thing I can say is that in that state, I wouldn't have known how to tell my toes from my fingers. He brought back one of his friends, who did his business and took off again. When Hamid returned, he was holding a shoebox that he put in the armoire with some bills inside. After that night, it happened several more times and every time in the same way. He went out. One of his "friends" arrived. We did the deed. His "friend" left and Hamid came back with bills that he put in the box.

Soon we moved because the neighbor started asking questions. We rented a room in a house where the owner didn't live on-site. We couldn't have found a better situation: she was in Sweden and returned only once a year.

It was in that house that I started to drink and smoke. And wear makeup. And sew myself djellabas that clung to my ass. And provoke Hamid's jealousy every chance I had.

Because that fucking box never filled. We never had enough money to buy the merchandise. And each time I asked him for an update, he had some new excuse.

It was also during that time that I stopped using soap down below. One day as we were arguing because the box had emptied once more, I made a vow. I vowed that Hamid would never dip his disgusting cock in anything but a disgusting pussy. That that was all he deserved. And all the others too. I never said it to him. And I never said it to anyone else.

After that, I started to do whatever I wanted. Just to provoke him. I let the grocer straddle me almost right under his nose. I let the grocer's employee have me when he came to change the bottle of gas. The watchman on the street. Everyone. Everyone with a stick between his legs could have me. And the more it annoyed that asshole, the happier it made me.

I finally asked him to stop bringing people to the house and instead to take me to the bar with him. I pushed and harassed him until he said yes. Once we had reached that stage, it was over between us. At the bar, I would wriggle myself in front of everything that moved, before his eyes and with a smile on my face. People thought he was my pimp. And really, what else was he? My husband? It had been a long time since anyone other than our families believed that.

*W*e lived for a long time this way. Our days were similar. I got up late. I spent the afternoon at the house watching television while he went off who knows where. When night fell, I got dressed and opened a bottle, which I sat in front of with my cigarettes. I started to get fat. I stopped cooking for myself but I blew up like a balloon. When he came back, we went out without speaking. We took a taxi and went to the bars. Eventually, he stopped coming with me. When I returned, I would put the money in the box and that was that.

Our routine was interrupted for a few months when I became pregnant with my daughter. But in total, we spent eight years like that. The will of God is unfathomable: while I'd never had a problem protecting myself, depending on the demands of my clients, it wasn't until I decided to start taking the pill that I became pregnant. I was twenty-six.

That pussy Hamid, when I told him that I was going to have a baby, wanted to run for his life. But I didn't give him the chance. I told him that I would go to the station and tell the police everything. And so he stayed. In any event, all his suspicions are bullshit. With the hair my daughter has, her father couldn't be anyone else.

A few days after my daughter was born, I handed her over to my mother. I couldn't take care of her, and Hamid couldn't stand that she was always crying for no reason. I didn't like when she suckled my breast, I didn't like changing her diapers. I couldn't even kiss her, can you imagine?

Two more years passed, we went to our parents' homes from time to time for parties and we acted as though everything was normal. Mouy, who sticks her nose in everything, especially when it has nothing to do with her, started questioning me one day about my green face, my greasy hair, my body she saw when we went to the hammam, which was starting to look more and more like harira.* She couldn't understand why my husband was making money and I was letting myself go. I didn't tell her anything, but still she ended her tirade with, "You should have listened to me..."

One day, Hamid got his next bright idea: he would secretly emigrate to Spain. It had been a long time since I'd stopped listening to him. I didn't even pretend to be interested, so little did I give a shit. He would speak about Spain more and more. Spain this, Spain that. And finally, he got serious. He suddenly stopped smoking joints. And he put all his energy into preparing his departure and gathering money for the smugglers. He would cross via Tangier, in a boat like the ones you see on the news. Full of Africans and other displaced people.

I'm sure he came up with terrible schemes to get that money. God only knows what he did. And it's none of my concern. I didn't realize that it was really happening until he called me one day from Spain to tell me that it had worked.

I don't wish for anyone to feel what I felt that day. It was as if you had kept the best bite of a tagine for the very end and someone came and grabbed it out of your fingers right at the moment when it was entering your mouth. You remain there, mouth open, fingers full of emptiness and a hollow taste in the back of your throat.

When he left, Mouy wanted for me to return and live with her but I didn't have the strength to see her and hear about it every day. So to have some peace and quiet, I told her that I had to stay in Casa to earn a bit of money and help Hamid, who had given away all his money to set himself up in Spain. She sighed even harder than usual and changed the subject.

One morning, when she called me to ask for the hundredth time if I would come to live with her, she told me before hanging up, "Be careful, my girl. Last night, I had a dream."

At the time, I never listened when she started telling her stories. "I dreamt of a white bird sitting on a bridge. It was giving a speech in front of an angry crowd."

"And?" I replied, sarcastic.

"I didn't like the head of that bird."

"Were you bothered because the bird was asking you for Samia's hand?" I added, laughing out loud.

"That's right, laugh and don't pay any mind to what I'm saying. Until something happens to you."

And she hung up.

Since that day, Mouy has scared me. I always suspected that she had premonitions but that was the proof. A few hours later, Hamid called me from Spain to talk to me about marrying someone else. When I saw the faqih* in town to ask him to decipher Mouy's dream for me, he understood immediately.

The white bird was Hamid. The speech was the announcement of the marriage. And the angry crowd was me. He didn't say things in such a straightforward way because faqihs always speak in code, but when I think about it, it's clear that that was it.

Hamid wanted for me to grant him the divorce so that he could marry over there and obtain his papers. As soon as I heard that, I told him to go to hell. I swore on my daughter's life and my mother's that I would never grant him the papers, not even if the earth split from the sky. After everything else, divorce was the last thing I needed.

Then I spoke to the girls about it, the friends I'd made since I started going out. That's when I met Samira, by the way. Even if we bicker from time to time, she and I get along well. She doesn't speak if she has nothing to say. She only acts like an idiot with that asshole cop.

The girls all told me to grant him the divorce so that my daughter might have a chance. Maybe if I help him out with this, he'll think of her once he has his papers? And he'll bring her to Spain? And she'll be able to grow up over there, go to school and build a future? And she'll get out of the shit we're in here?

In any event, I'm not stupid. I knew that one day or another he'd get the divorce, or he'd get the authorization to have a second wife. Even if it meant sending his baksheesh by boat.

So I said yes.

I made him swear on his mother's life that he would get papers for Samia when he had his own so she could go live with him. I obtained the divorce through spousal abandonment, and he remarried.

When I announced to my mother that I was divorced, I thought she was going to go insane.

"Are you out of your mind? Are you brain-dead?" she screamed into the telephone.

"Mouy, since the day you met Hamid, you've been saying that he's a loser, and now you're telling me I'm crazy for divorcing him?" I responded, before explaining to her why I did it.

"As usual, you're the one who knows best."

And she hung up on me.

*n*ot long after, I took Samia back. She was four years old. My mother didn't want to give her back to me. I don't know why I wanted her back. I had a bizarre feeling, as if two big warm hands were coming out of my stomach and reaching toward the little one to envelop her and put her back inside me.

To be honest, I already told you, I sort of regret not leaving her. She's starting to grow up and I'm afraid that some charitable soul will open her eyes to what's going on here. Or that she'll understand it on her own. And that she'll say things to arouse Mouy's suspicions.

I already get strange looks from that bitch teacher at her school. She always scrutinizes me from head to toe, as if she were seeing me for the first time every time.

Teachers look down on everyone. Especially women. They're not like that with men. When a father goes to speak to them, their arrogance flies out the window. I'm not afraid of them, or of anyone else. I'm polite when I go there and I speak to them with respect, lowering my head. And that's all.

Last year, Samia had a male teacher. It's simpler with male teachers, you can always come to an agreement. A man is a man. Once you know that he sees you through his zipper first, your troubles are gone. But women, they're all vipers.

The first time I met Samia's female teacher, at the beginning of the first term, she asked me what my husband did for work.

"God rest his soul. He died while she was still in my belly," I responded, gesturing at the little one, adopting a pitiful expression.

"God rest his soul," she sighed as if it had happened yesterday. "And what did he die of, the poor thing?" she added, clicking her tongue against her palate.

"A rafter fell on him, he was a construction foreman. It was a very difficult time. All that was left of him were crumbs."

She tried to look sympathetic, but I could see that she was clearly repulsed.

The little one, even if it bothers her when I tell stories, says nothing. She knows that I'll make up whatever nonsense necessary to have some peace and quiet. She speaks to her father from time to time. I gave him my Maroc Telecom number when Samia came back to live with me. And he calls her to see how she's doing.

Now, he lives in a city called Mataró and he's still waiting for his papers. I'm afraid of one thing: that that whore wife of his—a Moroccan from Meknes who does housework over there—will make things difficult for us. Or that she'll get pregnant and start to make demands. Or that she'll feed him some bullshit that will make him even more of an idiot than he already is. We have enough problems without her contributing to them!

So I keep a close eye on him. And since I know him better than anyone, I send him money and that's how I hold onto him. I know from experience that there's nothing he loves as much as money. Especially if he doesn't have to lift a finger for it. In his place, who would dare complain?

August

WEDNESDAY THE 18TH

I'm still in Berrechid. The clock changed again for Ramadan. I don't understand any of their stories anymore. When they said that they were moving to daylight saving time to save money, we didn't flinch. We even thought it was a good idea. Next they decided to do Ramadan hours because it's summer. I didn't really understand it, but why not? The problem is that apparently, after Ramadan, it'll be daylight saving time again, and after Eid, the clocks will go back again. Are they just fucking with us or what? Like we don't have anything better to do? Adjust your clock. Unadjust your clock! Readjust your clock. That's enough now!

Hamid, the guard, has just called me because he spoke to the neighbors' niece, who's back in Morocco for her work. She wants to meet with me as soon as possible.

"I told her that you would come in three or four days because her idea seemed interesting to me," Hamid announced, in the distant voice of someone who's calling from the bottom of a cave.

I couldn't hear well, and I answered him only half paying attention. I was watching a commercial on TV, thinking it was the best time of year to get a Méditel number. I know there are problems with the quality of their network, but why not? At least I can take advantage of the Ramadan promotion.

"Okay, that's fine," I responded, realizing that I didn't know what I was agreeing to, and I added: "Wait, what did you say, you told her I would come? Now you're telling her things on my behalf? Also, I can't come in three or four days. I'm busy."

That girl left me hanging for a month and now she wants me to drop everything? Well now it's her turn to wait! News story or not, those people who live abroad are all a bit nuts.

Right now, since it's summer, there are plenty of them here. All those emigrants who have houses in our neighborhood come back to spend Ramadan with their families. And I don't have to tell you how unbearable they are.

The other day, Khadija, the neighbor who has a house next to a power station and who lives in Belgium, left her son at our house because she had an errand to run and she wanted Mouy to look after him. Her son is a real spitfire. He wouldn't stop jumping. He flew from mattress to mattress. With his shoes on too. When my mother saw him, and when he wasn't expecting it, she tripped him, putting her right arm under the brat's legs at the very moment when he was launching for a jump. He rolled two or three times in the air before crashing onto the floor, like the divers you see on television. He was lucky there was a carpet.

Now, when his mother brings him to the house, he's more calm.

But in Belgium, his mother told us, the school sent the cops over to her house because she had hit him when he wasn't letting her clean in peace. The boy told the teacher and the teacher called the police. After that, how do you expect the kids to be normal?

So this crazy woman who wants to talk to me, I don't trust her.

"Tell her we'll meet after Eid, it's not so far from now," I said to Hamid.

"Ramadan started barely seven days ago. What are you talking about?"

Without waiting for my response, he continued: "Listen, this is between you two. I did my job giving you the message. I'll tell her about Eid and after that don't involve me anymore. What's in it for me in the end?"

And he hung up.

Mouy is hovering to try to guess who I'm talking to. I see her there but I let her turn in circles. That'll teach her to annoy me. Just now, she yelled at me to help her with the cleaning instead of sitting in front of the TV "like a couch potato."

"Who are you talking to?" she says, pretending not to really care about the answer and continuing to polish the wall, tracing zeros with her right hand.

God only knows what she's rubbing at. It's so clean that the only thing that could happen now is for the zellige to peel off onto her rag.

After so much practice, the lie comes out on its own. "No one, a guy who finds me work for different companies. He wants to place me with a woman who's looking for someone to organize her office."

"And that's how you talk to people who are doing you a favor? You speak as if I hadn't raised you properly," she says, turning her head to look at me.

Her hand has stopped swirling on the wall.

"Some favor. I give him my first two weeks of work to pay for his services. I'm not going to be a kiss-ass on top of it."

And we each return to our business. Me to my television. And her to her exercise.

September

The days go by. The wind blows and carries the days with it. Ramadan is over. Eid is over. Samia stayed with my mother. I went back to Casa.

I'm with Hamid in his shed and we're waiting for the neighbors' niece.

The day is almost over but it's still hot. And my djellaba is clinging to me. I tried pulling on the sides and the bottom to stretch the fabric for it to cling less, but it was no use. And sweat is turning the inside of my thighs all wet.

This summer doesn't want to end.

On the television, the king is meeting someone once again. He's in America. The French president—or whoever that gnome is—is standing next to him. Honestly, I wouldn't say no to a job like his. I'd get to travel, see the world, and give speeches on television.

But to tell the truth, if I were in his place, I wouldn't travel to those middle-of-nowhere places he normally goes. Now, he's in America, that's fine. But normally, you should see where he goes: Ben Guerir, Asilah, Ouarzazate. I want nothing to do with that. I would only go to high-class countries. Europe, Sweden, Brazil, Mexico. I'd leave the deserts to the beggars.

I would never wear the same outfit twice. And if I were hot like I am now, I wouldn't give a damn. I would walk around naked. And if someone had a problem with it, they could say it to my face. Or even better than walking around naked, I would install a portable AC on myself. I would put it over my head on a hat, it would keep me cool from morning to night and from my hair to my feet. And that would only be for when I want to move around. Because most of the time, I would sprawl out happily in front of the television, in a chilled room, and I wouldn't move until winter came back. Those who wished to see me would know where to find me.

"Phooey!" Hamid says, his eyes on the door where the curtain has fallen once again. "Am I going to spend my life keeping tabs on that fucking curtain?"

In this inferno, even the nail doesn't want the fabric rubbing against it.

"Let it go, there's nothing to do," I say, ashing into the little teacup placed in the middle of the table.

Hamid still has not fixed the table. Too bad for him. He'll regret it the day he tastes the tea's burning kiss on his thighs.

"The stench of armpit isn't enough for you? You want to add the cigarette stink too?" he says to me.

"Don't go getting all worked up with me," I answer, turning to look at him. "I know how to get worked up too."

And I place my elbows on my knees, spreading my legs because it's the only position where I get comfortable.

That's when she arrives. A skinny stick slides her head through the curtain and opens it with a fluid movement. A skinny stick with long disheveled hair at the end. Hamid told me she was the neighbor's niece but I hadn't imagined she would be so young. She's standing in front of the door and she's looking at us and smiling. Toothy grin. Horse's mouth! I look at her. She keeps smiling. I want to laugh. I had imagined her like Nassima el Hor*: pale, well padded, well dressed, coiffed, makeup done, put together. And a bit younger, of course; but at least a real journalist!

Instead, standing in front of me is a broom with its bristles dyed brown. She is so skinny that I'm afraid she's going to snap in two.

Hamid stands up. "Salaam, how are you?" he says, grabbing the curtain to hold it open for her and scratching his head. "It's hot in here."

That moron Hamid makes me want to laugh. As if he were caught in the act of having sex. He looks at me, then at her.

"I'm good, and you?" she responds, smiling at me.

And she reaches out her hand for me to shake it.

"Salaam, how's it going?"

"Good," I answer, handing her the tips of my fingers and looking at her out of the corner of my eye.

That pussy Hamid stays planted there, staring at us. I don't know what he's waiting for. He decides to go look for a chair outside. When he comes back, he sets it at the entrance and he grabs the shower curtain, which he passes over the rod to trap it there once and for all.

"So, how are you? Everything good? Your family's good? Your aunt, how is she? It's been a while since I've seen her. Hang on, I'll make some tea," Hamid says without pausing to take a breath.

And he gets up to fill a new teapot. I don't know what's gotten into him, he's acting strange. He can't find the sugar, he's looking for the tea, he finds it and loses it while he's cutting the mint. But he carries on talking at the same time. Horse Mouth is relaxed. From time to time, I lift my head from the screen toward one of them. But I don't speak. I don't know her and it's on her to begin, not me.

When he's done making the tea, he sits, he serves her a cup and he starts up his questions again. And once they know that everything is going well on both sides, they finally stop talking. I don't know how they managed it but in twenty minutes, they've tackled all the subjects on earth.

Her family is still in the Netherlands, and she's here with her aunt. Hassan, her aunt's husband, had a car accident. Hamid knows him and recommended a guy to fix his door. The guy inflated the price as much as possible because the other man was at fault and in any event, the insurance would pay. Her plane was late. The cold arrived early this year in the Netherlands.

Her speech is fluid. Unusual for emigrants. Normally it's like their tongue is in physical therapy: it needs crutches to get to the end of a phrase.

"I forgot my cigarettes, I'll go get them, be right back," she says to Hamid.

Hamid doesn't have any cigarettes but I know that he's waiting for me to offer her mine. I take my pack from the table and hand it to her, continuing to stare at the screen.

"That's nice of you, are you sure?" she asks me. I feel her look at me: "I'm always forgetting my cigarettes somewhere."

The king shakes hands. I nod my head to show that I heard what she said. That idiot Hamid responds, "It happens. The important thing is not to forget who you are."

Philosophy, that's just what we need! And he's serious too! Now he's posing like a stud, smiling, and he adds as if he were Imad Ntifi*: "So, your aunt told me you were working on something?"

"I'm working on a film. For the cinema. I'm a director."

She takes a long drag on her cigarette and continues. "I've already worked on several shorts and with directors who've made features."

And she adds, "This film I want to make, it's my first feature-length. I've almost finished writing the story. But I wanted to make sure that it's not too far off from reality. That's why I wanted to meet..."

And she turns her head toward me because she doesn't know my name.

Now that pisses me off! Can you believe that, a director who doesn't know the name of the person she's meeting with? I give her a dirty look, like I got up on the wrong side of the bed.

Once again, Hamid answers for me. "Jmiaa. Her name is Jmiaa."

"Great, you know what? I'm going to suggest something. If you're okay with it and you don't have anything to do right now, let's get out of this shed and go somewhere else. For a bit of fresh air."

And she gets up as if I'd said yes.

"Is there a place you like to go? Or else, we can just drive around if you prefer."

She's standing under the rod. I don't know what to do. To tell the truth, I like movies even more than television or the newspaper. She asks Hamid where the key to the car is. He takes it from the board where all the keys for the garage are and hands it to her. She takes it and turns to me. "Let's go?"

I get up and follow her. She gets into a crappy white Renault, starts the engine, and we leave the garage at full speed. The car sails through the packed Casa streets. Horse Mouth slaloms without slowing. As she drives, she searches all over and finally finds her cigarettes in the glove compartment. She sits back up, takes one, and throws the pack behind her. "I was so happy the day Hamid told me that you wanted to meet with me."

She turns her head toward me, smiling, and she changes gears with the hand holding her extinguished cigarette.

"Is there a particular place you'd like to go or is it all the same to you?"

"All the same."

Honestly, I could really go for a beer right now. She looks straight ahead and she says, "What we need in this weather is a nice cold beer."

And she adds, "That sounds good, right? What do you say?"

"I don't know. Whatever you want is fine by me."

"I know a good place, just here."

She hasn't even finished her sentence when the car takes a sharp left turn and launches between the palm trees lining the avenue. The cafés are packed. Around here, it's almost all students. Some are pretending to study and some don't bother. They hang around the park, trying to look like rockers with their crazy hairstyles. Mohawk here, mohawk there...And cock-a-doodle-doo here, cock-a-doodle-doo there. They're all the sons of bin-ou-bin.*

That's what we girls call them, the bin-ou-bin, the guys who don't know what they're doing with their lives. There are plenty around here. Respectable father figures who go to work every morning. They have a house, a car, children, but they have no life. They don't associate with the bearded men but all the same, they don't stray from the straight and narrow: no alcohol, no women, nothing.

They don't do it by choice, don't be mistaken. They do it because they don't have the balls to choose to be in one camp or the other. So, they do contradictory things. They cloister their wives at home but entrust them with their salaries at the end of the month. They forbid their daughters from going out at night but let them dress like Nancy Ajram* to go to school. They'd prefer that there not be girls like us at the entrance to the market—but when they pass, they lower their heads because they would never dare tell us to leave. That old crazy woman Mbarka knows how to handle them. There's only one thing you need to know about her, as we say between us, giggling: only half her brain functions. And not the good half. Since she's crazy, she can do what she likes. But I have an inkling she only pretends so that people leave her alone.

"Hey, I'm-afraid-of-my-own-shadow, look over here!" she shouts in the direction of the poor bin-ou-bin who doesn't yet know she's talking to him.

The entire neighborhood turns their head, men included, to see her lift her djellaba and thrust her pelvis forward in an obscene gesture. And immediately she bursts out laughing with her toothless mouth. We laugh too, while the guy lowers his head and flees the scene as if he hadn't seen anything.

"Okay, here we are."

Horse Mouth points at a bar I've never been inside but that I know.

We park opposite and go inside. She says hello to two or three people. There are men and women, it's mixed here. It's dark like in every bar, and there's Western music playing. She sits at a table in the back, past the first room and a second bar. It's like a bar within a bar.

We sit down. She gets up to buy cigarettes because she forgot hers in the car and she comes back
with a pack of Camels and places them on the table.

"I'm going to have a Spéciale. And you?"

"Me too."

How did I find myself here so quickly? I have
no idea.

She comes back with two beers in her hand. She
sits down and drinks directly from the bottle. She
lights another cigarette and starts to talk.

*T*here are a good dozen bottles in front of us.
And the butts of Camels and Marvels inter-
twined in the ashes. This girl is crazy. I underesti-
mated her, based on her mosquito size. But she can
hold her alcohol.

She told me some of her life story and a lot
about the film she's working on. I didn't catch
everything, but the important part is that she left
for the Netherlands when she was three and she's
lived over there ever since. She comes back to Morocco every summer. Now, she's going to produce
the film between the Netherlands and Morocco. It's
the story of a girl who earns her living as a pros-
titute. The girl, whom she hasn't named yet—but
she's deciding between Jamila and Hasna—meets
a man. They hit it off and get together, more or less.

They rob a jewelry store. And after they succeed, he rolls in the dough and takes off. And at the end there's a twist that I don't fully understand. And I don't remember anymore who comes out on top. A story like any other.

And she just wants to chat with me so I'll tell her what my life is like. That's all. And she has a small budget for it, but first and foremost, she wants to know what I think about it.

"About what?"

"About what I told you. The film, the story... Everything, really."

"It's good. It seems good to me. I don't know."

"Could it happen in real life? Could a girl fall in love with a guy and find herself robbing a jewelry store with him? Could she be scammed like that? What do you think? I don't know if it could really happen that way."

"..."

This girl might be crazy. She gathers her hair in a long ponytail at the top of her head. Some strands fall to the side.

I don't know why she's bothering with these questions. If you want to make a film, make a film and be done with it. She continues, "I'm also trying to imagine the ambiance. It would be filmed in my aunt's neighborhood. Next to the market, with the setting exactly the way it is. Maybe we'll change a few things, but we wouldn't touch the trash. Did you see how bustling it is over there? Hang on, I'm going to get another beer."

She weaves between the bin-ou-bin boys and comes back with the beers.

"Okay, you know what, in any case, we have time. We'll talk about it another day."

Honestly, she makes my head spin.

We stayed in the bar until they kicked us out. It must have been one in the morning. I don't know how many Spéciales we downed, but by the end beers covered the table.

Now, we're sitting in the car staring at the water. You can't tell where the sky ends and the sea begins. It's more distinct between the water and the sand. The waves, when they break, form huge braids of white wool. My nose is full of the smell of the sea. And I'm so drunk that I'm not even dizzy anymore.

Leaving the bar, Horse Mouth didn't take the road through the neighborhood. She turned left. I don't care. I've had so much to drink that I could go to Tangier if she wanted. She drove until we arrived at the corniche. There was almost no one in the streets. When we arrived, we drove slowly, looking at the seaside as we worked our way down the coast, until we reached Sidi Abderrahmane, directly across from the island.

We're not talking right now, but when we were at the bar, she talked a lot. I couldn't understand everything she said.

Basically, she came to Morocco to finish writing her story and to find locations to shoot. Now she'll return to the Netherlands to look for money from a producer to make the film. That part, for example, I didn't really understand.

If she doesn't have money, how is she going to make her film? And how has she almost finished writing it? And why does she want to keep the Casa streets as they are, why does she want everything to be as it is in real life? Why does she think people watch movies? To see the nasty reality or to get a change of pace and have a laugh?

Maybe it's the weed that's put those ideas in her head.

At the bar, while I was eating, I know she got up to smoke a few joints. She must have had two or three over the course of the night. When she came back her eyes were a bit glassy, completely calm. I know that look.

Also, she has a smoker's hands. Skinny and dark and a bit yellow at the tips. Now, she's just rolled another. The first one she's had in front of me. She hands it to me to light it.

"No, I don't smoke."

"You don't like it?" she says, lighting it and taking a long drag, her eyes half-closed, head slightly tilted back.

"I have a bad history with hashish. It's a long story," I tell her, seeing my husband's face in front of me.

"Mmmh..." she says, taking a puff.

I don't know if it's because the hashish is good or if it's in response to what I said. But I don't care. It's nice out, the drive was cool, and I feel good. We don't have music in the car. There's a radio but the FM button spins and spins. There's only the CD player, which works, but she doesn't have any CDs, she says.

"Next time, I'll bring Nass El Ghiwane.* Do you like them?"

"I don't know them. Is it chaabi*?"

"No. When you listen, you'll tell me if you like it. What kind of music do you like?"

Without thinking, I respond, "Najat Aatabou, do you know her?"

"Who doesn't know Najat Aatabou?"

She takes another drag and looks at the water. I light a cigarette.

When I think about it, in the end, I barely spoke that night. We ate, we drank, we drove. We talked a bit about Hamid. The neighborhood. And that's it. Leaving the bar, she took my number and asked if there was a good time for her to call me.

Then, she asked me to reflect on the film and whether I wanted to work with her or not. She also said that if I were to accept, we would talk about the money later.

And then she drove us here. That's all.

TUESDAY THE 21ST

When I'm lying in my bedroom, I never lock the door. It bothers me to have to get up every time one of the girls needs to borrow a tray, a bowl, or whatever else. Whoever wants something knocks, enters, and leaves again. And if they find the door locked, they come back later. And in their rooms, it's the same. We live like good neighbors.

The only problem with this system is that you can't control the comings and goings. Just now while I was sleeping, Samira came in, she woke me up and I can never get back to sleep. Samira is sitting on Samia's mattress. She's smoking a cigarette.

I'm not used to this room without my daughter yet. When I wake up, I turn to look at her mattress and find it empty. Halima is also gone. But in her case, it's for the best, I won't cry over her.

In the end, she got lucky. When Houcine told her to gather her things and clear out, she had an escape plan. Honestly, I get why Houcine fired her. She was taking up space for no reason. Imagine: no one even looked at her in the street! Or else just the perverts. She piqued their interest with her saintlike attitude, she must have reminded them of their sister or their mother or who knows.

Before I went to Berrechid, I spoke to Houcine about getting her out of my room. Frankly, I was very patient. I gave her time, I encouraged her to make herself at home. Anyone else wouldn't have waited a week to throw her out. Because having someone like that on your back all the time, it's impossible. It's true, she's nice and well mannered... But that's not the point. Always depressed, always hurting somewhere, always looking like a wounded dog...

The other day, before going to my mother's for Ramadan, I left her at my place but I told Houcine to get her out. In any event, I think he was already planning on it. She didn't earn enough with her jinxed face. And on top of it, I don't think he liked fucking her. That's what he does with the new girls. Under the guise of teaching them how to work. We're in charge of the theory and he takes care of the practice. Until he gets bored. To be honest, for a man who is supposed to be teaching you things, he doesn't really know what he's doing. It's only that idiot Hajar who doesn't realize it. When he calls her, she's thrilled. She thinks she's won something. Like when you collect Coca-Cola caps and once you have them all, you get a scooter.

He stopped hanging around me a long time ago and I like it better that way. Although, from time to time, he decides he wants to. He looks around, sprays himself here and there, like a dog when it wants to show the neighbor's dog that this is his territory.

I act with him like I do with all the others. If I feel like it, I act happy: I bray, I meow, I let him pull my hair or turn my ass red. Otherwise, I wait for it to pass. And my ass gets red anyway. Houcine isn't my type. He's too skinny, and with his patchwork of scars I worry he'll tear apart when he blows his load. I never did ask Halima what she thought of him. But to tell the truth, I don't care. All I care about is that he sent her packing.

So the other day, the boy who works in the drugstore came to change the lock on the armoire and give me a new key, I locked my things inside and I hit the road.

Samira told me what happened next. After Houcine spoke to her, Halima packed her bag and left. She didn't yell, she didn't cry. She did nothing: she just took her things, gave my keys back to Samira and left. Apparently, for some time, Halima had been visiting an elderly aunt on her father's side who lived in the old town, behind the clocktower. She lived alone, in a single room. That aunt—perhaps she was senile—agreed to see Halima despite what had happened with her husband. And Halima was happy because she felt she would go crazy doing this work.

You know, I think at the beginning she thought it would be easy. You show up, you do this for a little while, and then you move on to something else. The poor thing! If it were so simple, wouldn't there be more girls in the streets? Why does she think the girls smoke so many joints? Why does she think the girls self-medicate? Why any of it? It's because you need balls to be able to do this work. And not everyone has them.

Halima didn't last six months. Before leaving, she told Samira that she was going to live with her aunt and that she would work for a charity in her neighborhood. I don't know if she'd already found work or not.

"Actually…" I say, turning to Samira, "do you know where Halima's going to work?"

"Not exactly, but she talked about something connected to a religious organization with that nut they call Cheikh Yassine,* do you know him?"

"Yeah…"

"Or a charity for underprivileged children or something like that. Or both. I don't remember."

Samira was getting her wires crossed. But I didn't need to know any more than that. Basically, yet another clueless idea, the idea of someone who hasn't found anything better to do. Helping others! As if her own mess wasn't enough for her.

"And they're going to pay her?" I ask Samira.

"I don't know. She told me that she would also give private lessons for children in the neighborhood to help them with their homework."

Samira is sitting on the mattress and I stand to tidy up, to fold clothes and put them in the armoire.

I answer Samira while holding a sweater beneath my chin:

"Ha ha ha! Is she going to live in Maârif? Where does she think she'll have neighbors who'll have the money to pay for lessons in the old town?"

She really is an imbecile, that Halima.

"I don't know. But why not? If the prices are within their means, why not," Samira responds.

And she adds, "After all, she has somewhere to stay. She just has to make enough to buy food if she wants her aunt to keep her around. She can charge 400 rials per lesson. And do three lessons a day. Can't they both eat with 1200 rials per day? She and her aunt?"

"Yes, that's true," I answer.

And after a moment: "Yeah, but what if someone recognizes her over there? Someone who's been here?" I say, winking. "Will she give him lessons too?" I continue wriggling my ass toward Samira's giggling face.

Samira smacks me on the butt and we have a good laugh.

"Okay, forget about Halima. Where were you yesterday?" she asks, taking a drag.

"You know I like to disappear from time to time," I answer, evasive.

I'm not going to say anything to Samira about Horse Mouth. Samira is very suspicious. She mistrusts her own shadow, the poor thing. Sometimes it's helpful. But sometimes she overdoes it. Since I'm not really responding, Samira says to me, with an expression suggesting she thinks I had a good time the night before, "Sounds like Chaïba was involved."

A lie served on a silver platter. I couldn't have come up with anything better.

"Yes, that's it, I saw Bouchaïb."

I change the subject. "I'm going to the hammam. I didn't go yesterday. Want to come with me?"

"No, go without me. I'm on my period. In any case, I have to go," and she puts out her cigarette, exhaling the smoke lingering in her throat.

I pass in front of the Majestic before going to the hammam. Hamid isn't in his usual spot. From a distance I see his colleague washing a car. The car belongs to the Jewish woman opposite. Not the one who lost her daughter. The other one, who's always coming and going with her gym bag. It's like she's training for the Olympics, she exercises so much.

I continue on my way. Hamid will call me to hear about my outing with Horse Mouth, no doubt. I see right through him. Soon, he'll start talking about money. His little smiles to Horse Mouth and that tea he prepared for her and those cigarettes he wanted her to smoke, it's obvious he's buttering her up. He can't pull the wool over my eyes.

Honestly, I don't blame him. Everyone has to get theirs. I ask only one thing of him: that he take a second commission from the girl because if he thinks he's going to make money off of my back, we're going to have a problem.

In any case, I'm going to tell him so that everything is on the table: everyone for themselves.

I just got off the phone with Horse Mouth. And it was a whole ordeal to find my telephone, I won't bore you with the details. I've only just started hanging out with these film people and I'm already starting to lose it.

Just now, coming back from the baths, I started to wash my underwear, as usual. I put on a Najat song that I like.

The story is there's a girl who's sure her man is cheating on her. She realizes it through a glimmer in his gaze that betrays him. She's already given herself entirely to him, and she doesn't understand that he's been hooked by another. And she doesn't want to let him go because she's convinced they're meant to be together. So she tells this to everyone who will listen. Nothing out of the ordinary. But even so, I like this song. I listen to it often. And at full volume, as always.

It's good to have a place where you can do what you want without any busybodies meddling with your life. In my room, since my daughter and Halima left, there are only the walls, the television, the radio, and me. I do what I want. And I turn the volume all the way up. If I feel like it, I can crank it until my eardrums burst.

Anyway, just now, I put on the CD and started to do the washing. When the song began, I was singing over the basin. I had my underwear in my hands and I was rubbing the pairs gently against each other, humming to the music. At one point, I got up to dance a bit, because I love to dance. Especially when the rhythm is catchy, like this song. I sped up slightly and started to tap my feet on the ground, moving my hips from right to left. Dun, dun, dun.

The song sped up. The audience applauded Najat, unleashing a yell like the sound of a wave. And then, the guy meets his mistress.

It starts to heat up.

I followed the rhythm. Tapping harder and harder with my feet and swinging my hips farther and farther.

The girl looks the guy in the eyes and realizes that something is wrong.

I started to spin around, arms down at my sides, my feet continuing to strike the floor. Noisy taps. Booming loudly.

The girl tells him to do whatever he likes with her, she tells him that she belongs to him.

I followed the rhythm. I started to spin, spin, spin, like a top, arms wide like a flying bird, a pair of underwear in each hand.

The girl reminds him that she gave herself to him at his first smile. She tells him that she's going crazy.

I took off my scarf because it was starting to constrict my head. I tied it firmly around my pelvis, knotting it to one side. And my butt cheeks started to smack against each other like the wings of a butterfly.

The girl tells him that she's put all her trust in him.

I took out my clip to free my hair. I started to swing my head from right to left with my hair still wet from the bathwater. It sent drops rolling over my shoulders and splattering over the walls.

Then, the girl asks God's forgiveness for having strayed from the right path. She declares that her beauty and her beautiful black eyes are to blame for all of this.

And then I really let loose. That story wasn't my problem anymore. I felt the sudden urge to put a pair of underwear in my mouth. Just because. I bit down with all my teeth and plunged my hands into the basin to grab more. The bnader* started up. My ears became one with the bnader's taut skin.

I started hanging the underwear everywhere on me. From the scarf tied around my butt. Around my throat. On my dress too. I filled my mouth, I had underwear in my hands. Everywhere! In that moment, I no longer cared what the girl was saying. Let her shove it up her ass! I wanted to jump. The underwear swung from everywhere to the rhythm. My butt jiggled in the air. My head spun on my neck. My dress lifted up in rhythm with my feet, which had sent my sandals flying against the wall.

And amid all this commotion and celebration, I heard the telephone ring. I don't know how I managed to hear it. I pricked up my ears. I looked everywhere trying to follow the sound but I couldn't locate it.

Najat continued the celebration. I started to search under the cushions. I wet them with my hands. The underwear hanging from my thigh was dripping. My hair streamed over my arms.

I stopped, standing in the middle of the room. I looked around me, I saw the underwear in all four corners of the room, water on the walls and the mattress. As though a dog had been brought to the sea and then back to my place. As though someone had set the dog in the middle of the room and said:

"Here, go ahead, you can shake yourself out now."
That's what it looked like.

I was seized by a laughing fit! It sprung out of me like a firework. It didn't want to stop. One explosion after another. I laughed, laughed, laughed, like a crazy person. And speaking of crazy people, I was suddenly afraid of someone entering, someone seeing me like that and thinking I had gone insane. And that then I would be sent to Thirty-Six.* So I bounded toward the door to turn the key in the lock, my hair sticking straight up. I must have looked like a demon or Aïcha Kandicha.* It made me laugh even more. I leaned with my back against the door, and while I slid toward the floor, the fits of laughter came out relentlessly. I don't know how long I stayed like that, sitting on the ground.

Truly, I laughed until there was nothing left in me. And when the last hiccup had passed, I dried my tears and, between us, I thanked God for that moment. It had been a long time since I'd laughed like that. It's possible I had never laughed like that before.

People say it's not good to laugh so much. They say that when you laugh like that, Satan isn't far off. That he's taking advantage of your distraction to approach you. That he's ready to pounce.

What I think is that the people who say such things are just incredibly insecure. They do it because they're bored with their lives and want for everyone else to be like them: miserable.

Or else, they're paranoid and can't bear when someone laughs because they think it's about them.

Or else maybe the person who came up with that bullshit was just a moron with rotten teeth. And so now we have this fable because it was too late for him to fix his teeth. Stupid asshole!

In fact, you want to know the truth? The truth is that I believe it. Because of course Satan is nearby! If it's not me he's hovering over, then who is it?

*E*ventually I found the telephone as I tidied up the mess I had made. It was on a kitchen shelf. I didn't recognize the number on the screen. So I put the phone back in its place. If someone wants me, they can pay the money to send me a message.

Horse Mouth called back. She wanted to know if I had thought things over. She got straight to the point. I like direct people who speak without beating around the bush. What I had to do, she explained, was simple. I would sit with her for a few nights, talk, tell her what I was ready to tell without forcing anything. Just say what came to me. She would ask me questions, to which I would respond if I wanted and if I didn't have any issues with it. And if possible, I would introduce her to one or two of my friends. But only if it was possible, otherwise, it was no problem. She would be very happy already if

I agreed. She also told me that she had allotted seventy thousand rials of her film budget for me. She said that she took it out of her own pocket. As if it made a difference to me where it came from. The important thing is that there was money, right?

Before she called me, I already knew that I'd say yes. I knew it from the moment I met her in the shed. Going to the bar only confirmed that I would work with her. I knew that what she would ask me would be easy enough. What would we do together? We'd chat and down a few beers? We'd drive through the neighborhood when people are normally asleep? I would tell her stories and she would use them to make her own? If that was it, I could help her out with a different film every week if she wanted.

When we spoke about money, I didn't try to negotiate. At first because when she called, I was with Samira and I hadn't told her anything about it. Also because I planned to smoke and drink for free the entire time she was here. Trust me, I'd get her to double her budget.

THURSDAY THE 30TH

Between the other day and now, Horse Mouth and I have gone out several times. Four or five times, I can't remember. Mostly at night. To that place we went the first time. It's called La Mygale.

Each time, we had a good laugh and I told her some of the stories of my life. We drove around the neighborhood. I showed her the girls from a distance. I told her about Samira's asshole Aziz. I told her about Halima. That was my job: help her so that she could finish writing her story. Piece of cake.

Now she's in the Netherlands. She left yesterday. She's going to sign a contract with the people who will give her the money to make her film. And she'll come back once it's ready. I don't know when, but it shouldn't take too long. She told me that she would call me when she was back. She agreed that I could come for a day while they were filming. Based on what I know of her now, she's a woman of her word. She's going to follow through.

In the meantime, I've resumed my normal life. Nothing new.

Except that Chaïba is often around and there are a few ripples between us now.

Since I was busy with the Horse the past few days, I didn't have time for him. And he didn't like that. And I don't like when people meddle in my life. Even if that person is Chaïba and I've known him forever.

The day before yesterday, for example, I was with Horse Mouth and Chaïba called me so we could meet up. He had already tried calling twice at a bad time when I wasn't free. I think it bothered him that I didn't hustle over as soon as he called the first time, as if I didn't have a life of my own.

He gave me a hard time before that too. During Ramadan, he had called me so we could meet up while I was still in Berrechid. He usually disappears during Ramadan. He stays shut away in his house. He can't handle the fast: no cigarettes, no coffee, no alcohol, and he's worthless. But when he called me, he wanted me to come and see him. Who knows, maybe he was sick of his wife and his three monkey children. Honestly, I feel sorry for him. I saw them in town one day. They were with him in the car and they were jumping around in the back. When they drove past me, Bouchaïb had turned toward them and he was yelling at them. His wife, who was in the passenger seat, was staring straight ahead with her lips pursed. She's got one of those faces. Let's just say I understand why he spends his time out of the house.

Anyway, I wasn't available to see him, but when I came back to Casablanca, I returned his call. We saw each other. We went out. We were at Atomic, another bar he takes me to sometimes. That night, he hadn't brought those two idiots Saïd and Belaïd. We were sitting at the back of the room. The two of us, it was nice.

The entire night, we drank, we laughed, we ate. He had brought me a scarf, red and yellow. A beautiful scarf. Later, we were at my place. We left his car by the bar and we went back on foot. We were loud in the street and we weren't walking very straight. Once at my building, we went up the stairs and down the hallway, talking and laughing. We were all worked up, we started to touch each other.

At the second floor, he was so excited that he wanted to have me on the spot. He had lowered his zipper and when I pushed him away, telling him to wait until we were inside, he decided to piss in the hallway. It was good timing, we weren't far from Okraïcha's door. I signaled with my eyes toward the door so that he would relieve himself on it. As soon as he finished, I quickly pulled him away in case she heard us and came out in a rage. Even at two in the morning, you never know. We had a good laugh about it.

We continued up the stairs, banging against the walls to the right and the left, partly because we were drunk and partly because we weren't looking in front of us, too busy sliding our hands under each other's clothes. Once we were in my room, we didn't even make it to the mattress. I'll admit that I was really turned on too. He grabbed me when the door had barely closed, we melded together like dough and we threw ourselves onto the floor, rolling around, like how it used to be with my husband when we were young.

When we finished, we sat on the rug with our clothes and our hair disheveled, smoking a cigarette.

And then we were hungry. Ravenously hungry. I made eggs with olive oil, which we gorged on with cold bread. The eggs gave him the strength to get up, haphazardly. He mostly tucked his shirt into his pants, stood, and took off stumbling.

He came back five minutes later. I don't think he'd reached the bottom of the stairs before he'd decided to come back.

When he knocked, I was already beached on my mattress, in a djellaba because I hadn't managed to put on my nightshirt. I stood up, running my hands over my hair to smooth it before opening the door. I found him leaning against the wooden frame, hunched slightly forward. He was having trouble standing up straight. Some of his shirt had come out of his pants. His enormous lips were hanging open and I found him utterly ordinary. I couldn't stand him.

"What did you forget?" I asked, turning back toward the room to see if I could find anything.

"I forgot the most important thing."

He made a half attempt at a smile, put his hand in his right pants pocket, and handed me some crumpled bills. I couldn't stand it.

October

FRIDAY THE 19TH

Hamid (my husband, not the moron from the garage) crawled out of the hole he had been sucked into. It had been a while since I'd heard news from him. When I saw all those numbers on the screen, I knew that it was an international call. I thought it was Horse Mouth calling to give me an update.

When I answered, it was him. He needed 1.5 million dirhams, he said. He had found a guy who could draw up his papers quickly, for three million. But he couldn't come up with the money because of the economic crisis over there. He said that times were tough. I don't know why he was telling me about his life as if I were his mother or something. Times are tough for him, okay, what do I care?

First of all, even if I wanted to, where would I get 1.5 million from? Everything seems simple to him. He calls, he asks for 15 thousand dirhams, and then he goes and farts around in front of a latte while waiting for it to arrive. Does he think I birth money? That each month, instead of having my period, dirhams line my underwear?

The only effort he makes is walking the two hundred yards between him and the grocery store* where I send the money. And sometimes it's that whore who goes to get it for him.

What made me laugh is that he had already figured out the other half. I'm sure his wife gave it to him. But anyway, that's not my problem and I don't have time for it now. I have to get to work.

It's eleven in the morning and I haven't stepped a foot outside today. It's not very nice out. I quickly put away the breakfast crepes, I put the plate of olive oil on the shelf, I put on my djellaba and I go out.

This hangover every morning, I'm sick of it. It only goes away when I drink. You'll say, that's better than those disgusting pills Rabia takes. Most of the time, she doesn't remember anything that she's done. She doesn't even know where she spends her money.

I circumvent the garage so that I don't have to pass in front of it. I have no desire to run into Hamid. He wants part of the money Horse Mouth gave me. Even though I've already told him to figure it out with her, and even though he has no idea what I've made, he wants his piece.

Maybe he regrets not having taken more from Horse Mouth. Or maybe he milked her good but he'd decided that two milk cows are better than one. Who knows.

The girls are on the stairs. Samira isn't there. She's probably already left with someone. They're sitting and talking about all the prices that have gone up: flour, tea, tomatoes. When they have nothing left to say on the subject, they go quiet. Those who have cigarettes smoke them.

Now, one of them is taking about the taxi strike. They have been parading through the streets on Sunday, leaning on their wailing horns because— apparently—they don't care for the new road safety rules. No one answers her. Because in fact, nobody cares. It's not the horns that are going to make the clients disappear. And on top of it, none of us have ever held a steering wheel in our lives.

So, they talk about cigarettes, which they say are going to become even more expensive, and the price of beer, which has gone up this summer. They're starting to drive me crazy.

If it weren't so early, I would have had something to drink. I'm sick of it.

"Are you going to do a full recap of the news, or what?"

"What's up with you? Having a bad hair day?" responds Hajar, insinuating that I'm only complaining because I got up on the wrong side of the bed.

She stares me down. What business is it of hers? She might be in a bad mood, but mine is far worse.

"You think you can talk to me like that? Who do you think you are?" I say.

"Your mother! Who do you think?"

And then we all get up at once. I jump on her and try to rip out her mane of hair. Her scarf is in my hands. Her scarf and a good clump of hair. She scratches my face. And in less than two seconds, the others have separated us.

That whore knows she has to be the one to move and she stumbles up with her friend, who follows her to go sit under the porch of the store opposite. As they go, they keep turning back to insult me.

The others—who stayed by my side—tell her she'd be better off keeping her mouth shut. She scratched my temple, that whore. And with her lioness nails, she tore the skin. I'm bleeding. What a shitty day!

The girls look around to see if Houcine is nearby. Although he usually stays out of our business, he can't stand it when we cause a spectacle in the street. If he had seen us, he would have gotten his fist involved. And today, I am not in the mood to keep quiet, not for a fist or for anything else. I would have smacked him too and then who knows what kind of mess I'd be in.

But she was asking for it. She's been pissing me off for a while now, and I'm mad at myself for not mangling her face.

You know what she did the other day? The day when I was with Horse Mouth and I didn't answer Chaïba's call? She clung to him until he finally went with her. Even though she knows perfectly well that he's mine. And that son of a whore only went with her to piss me off. He couldn't stand that I didn't pick up, that baby. And he knew perfectly well that it would get back to me. When I called him, he didn't answer and he never even called me back.

She thinks that he went with her because of her beautiful eyes... Dirty whore! But forget her. And forget him too. Let him do the rounds of all those other whores and when he's done and comes crying back to me, we'll just see what happens. We'll see which one of us doesn't pick up the phone.

2011

January

THURSDAY THE 20TH

I'm sitting by the window in my room. It's the end of the afternoon and the window's closed because it's cold. It might rain today.

From here, I can see glimpses of sky and several clouds. On the mattress to my right is a page from a newspaper to catch the shells of the pepitas as I eat. I've had so much practice that I don't even need to look at the page to know they're landing on it. Right on the head of Ben Ali, the Tunisian president. Serves him right! I don't care for that thief.

In the street, I see that crazy girl Anissa fighting with her jinns. She came back to the area a few days ago. I'm waiting for Horse Mouth, who should be here any minute now. She'll call me when she's out front. I hadn't heard from her since she left for the Netherlands in September or October.

I'm bored. I'm tired of being bored. And I'm tired of being alone and cycling through the problems tangled up in my head like the yarn in a ball of wool. It's been years since I've been able to distinguish one day from the next, so much do they resemble each other, and now, in less than three months, everything's gotten mixed up.

First, the event that started it all, is that I was hit by a motorcycle. Because of some idiot, I was in the hospital for three weeks.

I was walking peacefully in the street with Samira, I had just passed the market to go to the liquor store that is next to the call shop. It was the beginning of the afternoon. We were on the sidewalk and before we crossed, we slid between two cars to reach the street. I was in front, Samira behind. We were talking. Maybe you think that I turned toward her as I was crossing and so I didn't see the motorcycle coming? Or else that I was drunk and in the haze of my intoxication I didn't see what was happening? Well you would be wrong. No, I was walking and just as I was about to cross, I looked left where the cars were coming from and I stepped onto the road. Samira didn't have the time to cry out before I was struck by that asshole going the other way. He was going the wrong way and driving at full speed.

As soon as he got up, he mounted his motorcycle and disappeared as quickly as he'd appeared.

Do you think anyone went to follow him? Or came to see whether he'd left me dead or alive? We were in front of a café, and the men sitting at their tables who had witnessed the scene wedged even farther into their seats. Sipped their coffees. Free show, what more could you ask for?

Samira started to scream, the passersby leaned over to see what all the fuss was about. I sat up, glanced at my right leg, touched my bleeding skull, and fainted.

When I came to, I was still in the street. They had carried me to the sidewalk. Samira was running her hand over my face with water. My right shin was wrapped in a cloth. I think it was my scarf.

We were waiting for the ambulance that that moron Aziz had called for us. At least he was good for something. And he must have decent connections because the ambulance was there in less than a half hour. It was a shitty ambulance, an old white model, a station wagon. Samira got in with me and we headed for the hospital.

They shaved part of my skull and started to stitch me up, they did X-rays of my head, my hips and my legs. In the end, I was lucky, because outside of the wound on my head, I only broke part of my leg, just above the ankle. Two fractures that they had to operate on. That's why I stayed there for three weeks.

But I was very lucky: they were able to operate on me right away. And it went well. I didn't even have those skewers that run down your legs like my neighbor in the next bed over.

In the room where they put me, there were six of us. One of the women had had the same operation as me. Except she had arrived at the hospital six months prior. They weren't able to do the operation then because her skin was blistering. So they sent her back home and she wallowed there on her back for six months before they would touch her. And the day they opened her up, they found a real mess inside! She told me this story the day when Samira, Fouzia, and Rabia came to see me. All three at once! They brought oranges, bananas, apples, yogurts, dates. As if it were a banquet.

It must have been three or four in the afternoon. They had walked through the hallways wrangling chairs so they could all sit. And they had paid off the head nurse—people called her Madame Touria—so that she'd leave us alone even if we got a bit noisy. She's the one who was there when I was admitted, and Samira had already given her a little something.

Anyway, the girls came in and sat to the right of the bed, in a line. Behind them was the window. Those bastards, of course they put me in a room where you could die of cold. From my bed, to my left, I could see the gaping hole that served as the door to the room. The wooden panels had been torn off long ago. There was no curtain separating me from the women next to me. And you could hear everything that happened in the hallway. How do they expect you to recover in a place like that?

Well, none of that stopped us from making ourselves at home, to be honest. We were sitting and telling stories in turn. I hadn't had a chance to tell them who I had seen on the television just before my accident. On the *Moukhtafoune* program, the one where they investigate missing people, there was the story of a guy who had asked them to search for his wife's sister. He told them she had psychological problems. The channel had been contacted by the Tit Mellil community center. The human garbage dump at the outskirts of Casa. For some time they'd had a patient who looked like the girl in the photo and when they called the station, it turned out to be her.

They filmed the moments when they brought her out of the center and when she was reunited with her family. When the camera entered the house, where a ton of people were waiting, the TV guys realized there was a problem. There were people arguing.

"I love when it spirals out of control like that," said Fouzia. "When family gets involved, chaos always breaks loose sooner or later."

The journalists started to ask questions to find out what exactly was going on. It turned out that the stepbrother who had made the call had done it without asking his wife and her brother. And those two scumbags, all while saying that they were very happy to see her again, were also saying that they didn't have anyone to look after her and that it would pose a problem for them to keep her in the family. That they were afraid she would jump out the window.

"Afraid she'd jump out the window? Seriously? In my opinion, as soon as the camera's gone, they'll open the windows wide to 'have a breath of fresh air,'" said Samira, snorting out of her nose like a horse to show that she wasn't fooled.

They spoke of the inheritance that followed their mother's death. Bizarrely, they were vague about the portion intended for the sick girl, who throughout the entire incident was unaware of what was going on around her. As if none of it involved her. In the end, the brother said that he would keep her at his house. And the episode ended there.

"Yeah, I know where that inheritance money went," said Fouzia.

Her right wrist spun as if she were turning on a faucet and then she slid it toward the pocket of her djellaba to catch the imaginary loot.

"Yeah," sighed Samira, "we all know where the money went. But as for the poor girl, that's another story."

"Well, I have an idea," I said with a big grin.

And so as not to prolong the suspense too much, I continued immediately:

"She's that crazy girl Anissa. During the entire show, I was looking at her and couldn't believe my eyes. When I recovered from the shock, I laughed for a long time. I spend all my free time staring at the screen and when I finally recognize someone on the television, of course it's a crazy person."

And the girls laughed and the neighbors laughed too. My leg hurt and I asked Samira to turn me onto my right side, apologizing to my neighbor for turning my back to her. Samira propped me on the cushions and as she was arranging my nightshirt, she lifted her head toward the girls and added, "While we're telling stories, have Jmiaa and I ever told you this one?"

And she told them, lowering her voice a bit, about a night when something too funny happened to us. It was a long time ago, I don't even remember when. Fouzia and Rabia hadn't heard this one before. One night, we had been picked up late. The back of the van driving us to the station was jam-packed. At one point, the van pulled over to the right and stopped. The door opened and there in front of us, we saw three young guys, well dressed, standing there yelling at the cops. The cops didn't know what to do. and they were saying, looking at the one of the three who seemed to be the leader, "Yes chief, yes chief."

"Are you stupid or something? You don't have anything better to do tonight than pick up these pieces of shit?" said the oldest of the young guys, the chief.

And to better imitate the policeman, Samira placed her finger under her nose like a mustache and raised her tone.

"Okay, okay, chief. We'll let them go right away, chief," said one of the idiots in uniform without asking why.

"Go and run to the square over there instead of hanging around here. There are bottles flying, there's blood."

Once we got out, those of us who'd been in the van didn't know what to do. There were two or three who bolted without looking back. And Samira and I, along with the others, we stood there staring at the chief and his two lackeys waiting for them to tell us what to do.

"So, what did you do?" asked Fouzia.

"Well, the three young guys took their pick," I answered, laughing. "And she and I were up for grabs."

"Wait, I'm the one telling the story," Samira said, cutting me off and forgetting to lower her voice. "So, they brought us to a house that looked like a palace. With a pool, a giant living room as big as the square with the pigeons. They brought out bottles. You remember?" she asked, turning toward me. "Those young guys weren't chiefs any more than we were men. What a night!"

And then, as we carried on laughing, I heard a voice I knew too well say behind me:

"Salaam alaykoum."

My blood boiled. Mouy. Mouy had come.

How long had she been standing at the door? What exactly had she heard? How had she managed to find me? I don't know. What I do know is that Mouy approached and sat down in the chair Samira offered to her, thanking her with a nod of her chin. And she acted as if she hadn't noticed that Samira was now left standing. Samia was with her. She was holding her hand. She gave me a kiss and squeezed me in her arms. I think she had been afraid when she heard that her mother had been in an accident.

Fouzia and Rabia took advantage of that moment to get up and say goodbye. Passing in front of Mouy, they nodded at her. Mouy glared back, scrutinizing them from head to toe. If I had been standing, my legs would have given way beneath me. Instead, I sank into my mattress as one might fall into a well. I thought I was done for.

That was essentially the case.

Mouy put in her five minutes, staring straight ahead. She sat upright in the chair. She lifted the sheet with the tip of her fingers to see what was underneath. She asked two or three minor questions. And she left, taking Samia with her. And leaving behind her a small bag in which were two nightshirts, one of hers and one of Samia's, cakes, a djellaba, and a scarf.

I haven't seen her since. And I haven't spoken to her either. I haven't been able to call her. And she hasn't called me.

How did she know that I was there? It's a ridiculous story.

When they admitted me to urgent care, the nurse Touria took my things while the doctor ran some tests. As luck would have it, my mother chose that precise moment to call. Luck, and maybe she'd also had another one of her dreams. Who knows.

While the doctors examined me, the nurse was in an adjoining room, my things placed next to her. My telephone rang for a long time, it hurt Touria's ears and she grabbed it to turn it off. She saw "Mouy" on the screen and she answered.

That's how life goes sometimes. You don't know why things happen but they happen. How would the nurse have known that a Jmiaa Bent Larbi* would have purposely not told her mother that she had just been mowed down? How? If it had been at any other moment than in the urgent care unit, or just a few days later, when she knew who she was dealing with, surely she would not have said anything to her. It was unlucky, that's all.

Horse Mouth is downstairs. I saw her char-
iot arrive before she called me. I put on my
red djellaba because it's hot out, and I grabbed my
cane. It's impossible to go down the stairs without it.
Honestly, I can't really manage these three flights of
stairs anymore. When I was released from the hospital, even with Samira's help, it took me an hour to
walk up them. Now, things are better. My leg has
healed somewhat thanks to the gymnastics they've
got me doing, but it's hard. Even though I've lost
weight.

Yes, I've lost weight.

One afternoon—I had just gotten back from the
hospital—I was tired of lying down in front of the
television, watching those images flicking by one
after another on an endless loop. I wanted to get up
to grab the envelope of photos in my armoire and
look through them. I leaned on my right elbow to get
up, I took my cane with the other hand, and when I
tried to stand up, I felt the weight of my butt pulling me down toward the mattress, like a magnet.
Impossible to rise. I was pulling one way and it was
pulling the other.

That's when I realized that for a good month now
I'd only been using two parts of myself: my right
hand and my mouth. The former to flip through

channels and bring things to my mouth. Anything: cakes, chips, bread, peanuts, pepitas. And the latter to chew and make comments about what was on the screen. And right then, I was afraid.

My butt sank so far into the mattress that I thought I was glued to the spot. If I let my butt have its way, how would I live? And what would I do about my husband on the other side of the sea, and my mother, and the shitty rent payments that were adding up, and the cigarettes I needed? And all the rest. The medication, the alcohol, Houcine, food. What was I going to do about that?

It wasn't hard to lose weight. Each time I wanted to put something in my mouth, Anissa appeared in front of my eyes. Wandering in the street, talking and laughing to herself. I couldn't fathom that my butt, which had helped me to live all this time, would also be the thing that led to my downfall.

No matter what I had in my hand, I would drop it abruptly onto the table. Sometimes, I would throw it down so forcefully that it would bounce to the floor. Samira was constantly shouting because I was throwing everything on the ground. So I stopped. Not because of Samira and her diatribes. But because I was afraid that throwing things with no self-control was the beginning of madness. I stayed in my spot watching television and taking pills without eating.

If I hadn't been sick, I would never have lost those thirty or forty pounds. I've never weighed myself. Generally, I know I've gotten bigger when I have to really force my djellaba over the top of my hips. Simple. And now, I know that I've gotten much thinner because I had to bring my djellabas to the tailor for him to take them in.

It takes me almost ten minutes to go down the stairs. Horse Mouth doesn't know yet that I was hit straight on by that stupid motorcycle.

She's parked in front of the building, head down, rolling a joint. I open the door. She looks at me, spreading her lips over her big teeth:

"Salaam alaykoum," she says, lifting her head.

I smile back and bend down to enter the car, my healthy leg first. I lean on the roof of the car to keep my balance. I sit down and place my cane to my left. I grab my right leg with my two hands around the knee and I pull it into the car. I make an effort not to breathe too hard.

"Alaykoum salaam," I say to her as if everything is fine, holding out my hand for her to shake, "long time no see."

She says nothing. She places her joint in a small compartment under the radio. She glances at my leg and my cane. I don't know what's going through her head but it's painful to see. It looks like she's fallen ill. Her mouth is still pulled toward her ears but she's not smiling anymore. She says, half-worried, half-curious, "Aye, aye, aye, aye, are you okay?"

She hasn't even seen my knee yet. Where the scar is, the skin is swollen, blue and thin like puff pastry. And the scar is long, fat and violet.

Horse Mouth snorts, shaking her head quickly from left to right, and since I don't respond to her question, she adds, "What happened to you?"

If I were in the mood, I would have made up some wild story. But I'm already starting to sweat and I don't really feel like laughing. I don't know why I told her we could meet.

"I was hit by a motorcycle. A guy ran into me and then took off."

"Pffft, I was afraid. I thought you'd been beaten up in a brawl," she responds, bringing her hand to her chest, relieved.

"A brawl?" I ask. "What do you take me for, a chemkara*?"

Honestly, that could easily have been the case, or something worse, who knows? But I don't tell her that.

"Sorry. It's just that in the screenplay, there's a brawl that takes a bad turn. I think I got overexcited from being so inside the story. But what happened exactly?"

"A guy on a motorcycle ran into me and fled the scene. I had to have surgery, but now I'm okay. And you, how are you?" I sulk.

She's not going to insist anymore, I know her now. She hesitates but eventually responds, "Things are good. Fine."

She doesn't know what to say.

To be honest I'm sick of it. I'm sweating despite the cold and this djellaba is bothering me. I'm sick of this leg. And I'm sick of this cane. And these pills, I don't think they're working on me anymore. I have to take something or I'm going to lose it.

She goes straight to the bar. We're in front of the door. The car clock shows five in the evening.

We cross the street and it takes us some time. We sit in the front room. Horse Mouth calls the server and she orders "two Spéciales, my brother," without asking what I want.

It bothers me. I've already lit a cigarette and in four puffs, I'm almost halfway through.

"No, I'm not drinking anything," I say to the server, wagging my index finger no.

I turn toward her and say: "I'm on medication. I can't drink."

"Let's go then," and without waiting, she yells toward the server: "Si Mohamed!* Sorry, cancel the order. We forgot something."

It's a lie that I can't drink. But I've started to be careful. Otherwise, this could all end badly. I've set myself a limit: not a drop touches my lips before six. I spend the day waiting for six o'clock so that I can pour the liquid down my throat, onto my tongue. And the problem is that once I've had a drop, my body demands more. And soon, I can't control myself anymore. I drink until I'm knocked out. All alone in my room. Or with Samira if she's not working.

You know, the days go by slowly when you stay sitting in the same room having a conversation with yourself. Samira comes to see me, the other girls too from time to time, but everyone has their own life to live. People are afraid you'll rub off on them. But to find yourself alone, again, that's not the real problem. The real problem is money. And the problems that arise when you don't have it. I need to get myself back on the stairs soon because Houcine is starting to lose his patience with how little I'm paying him right now.

He hasn't asked me for anything. And he hasn't come to see me. But I can sense his tension, even from afar. You never hear me talk about him because he and I don't have a problem. But we have a good relationship because I play by the rules, and even when I'm sick, I honor my commitments. At the end of each month, I find him somewhere, I give him money, and he puts it in his pocket and leaves until the next time.

At the beginning, it bothered me. He would watch over me like death at the bedside of the sick. He was afraid I was trying to dodge him. After each client, I would find him behind me. As if making sure I wasn't trying to rip him off. And then when he understood that I wasn't causing any trouble, he returned to his business. I'll admit that more than once I thought of taking off and ditching him. But then, each time, something happened to make me change my mind. Like this one day, there was a guy who had done his business and then thought he could go back to his life, skipping over the small matter of paying up. In my room, in an attempt to take care of it without causing a scene, I told him it would be better for him to hand it over now before he regretted it. He responded, puffing out his chest: "Oh yeah? And what are you going to do about it if I don't cough it up?"

"You don't want to know what I'm going to do if you don't cough it up."

"Yeah, sure. Go on then, show me," he said, pulling up his pants.

And he opened the door, looking at me from above, like the hero in an American movie. I gave him a weak "go fuck yourself" and followed him out, quickly. I won't tell you how he ended up, our hero. Before reaching my room, I had seen Houcine leaning against a car joking around with a man, a Spanish guy—José Lechetta they called him. He's missing a piece of his tongue. Apparently some chick cut it off with a razor. I'm not telling you these details to scare you, only to give you an idea of the kind of guys Houcine keeps company with.

So, that moron who didn't want to pay, he walked out without wondering why I hadn't caused a scene. He was just happy to be out of my bedroom with his pockets as full as his balls were empty. I promise you, that day, the guy regretted all that liquid: the liquid he spurted onto my mattress, the liquid assets he guarded in his pockets, and what came out of his nose when Houcine and his friend beat him up opposite the guy selling donuts.

Even so, he was lucky, because Houcine and his buddy, they gave him a break, offering each other the choice cuts. Here, you take the thigh, it's nice and tender. No, no, you have the honor, you're my guest today. The guy emerged from that impromptu celebration like a piece of bone in a chicken tagine: all gnawed on.

And so, every time I think I'm going to ditch him, and even though Houcine taxes me as much as the State does on alcohol, I always reconsider, because with him at least I can have peace of mind. What bothers me is that right now I'm broke. My savings aren't infinite. And all that alcohol isn't going to help me get back on my feet.

The other morning, I was so wasted when I went to sleep that I woke up on the rug. I had fallen from my bed in the night and I hadn't even realized. When I woke up, I had two open stitches on my leg. I was lucky that day. The wound could have popped open like a zipper.

When I saw myself in that state, I decided to do something. So now, I drink every night but only a little. It's the only trick I've found that works. That and the pills, of course. They calm the nerves but let me tell you, they also quench my thirst. They cloud my mind a bit, but they work. So, tonight, Horse Mouth or no Horse Mouth, I refuse to drink before six o'clock.

"Let's take a little drive along the coast instead?" she says to me, opening the door.

I'm tired of all of it. I don't want to open my mouth, not even to ask her to bring me back home.

We arrive at the beach right at sunset. She parks the car next to Sidi Abderrahmane and she retrieves the little joint she'd stashed under the radio.

I hand her my lighter because I have no desire to watch her writhe around in every direction looking for her own. Rather than taking it, she hands me the joint for me to light it. Then she takes it back, saying, "I forgot you don't smoke."

Horse Mouth turns toward me and says, smiling, happy, "I got the money. All the money I asked for."

And after a long puff, she adds, "We start filming at the beginning of April."

"That's great. Will you stay here until then?"

Rain starts to fall in fine tiny drops. I lower the window to feel the sea. It's strange, I'm not dizzy. And it's strange, in this moment, I see the world through the eyes of a sick person. As if I were going to die.

Horse Mouth, spitting out the tobacco sticking to the end of her tongue, responds, "No, I'm leaving for two weeks in March."

I had forgotten that I had asked her a question. From the ground, she picks up the enormous bota bag she uses as a purse. It's the same color as her jacket. And her shoes. Since the first time I met her, she's worn the same clothes: the same jacket, the same blue jeans, the same pale T-shirt and the same leather boots. They're falling apart and the tongues hang down on each side of her foot. They're terrible, but to each her own.

She riffles through her bag for something, pushing around the objects inside.

She takes out a parcel and hands it to me. It's covered in shiny black wrapping paper, with red and yellow flowers. And a gold ribbon wrapped around it.

"What is it?"

She's annoying me. I'm sick of her smile and her giant mouth.

"Just a little something. Take it. Open it."

She adds, "I wanted to thank you. What you told me really helped me to write the story."

The paper refuses to rip. It's not normal wrapping paper. It's as if it were made out of plastic. I pull on the gold ribbon. It doesn't want to open either. Oh well. I'm pissed off. I put the paper in my mouth and try to tear with my teeth as hard as I can. A piece of the wrapping gets stuck between my teeth. I spit it out the window. Fuck, what moron makes wrapping paper like this? I throw the shitty package in front of me. It knocks against the glove compartment before falling to the ground at my feet.

"Fuck, I'm sick of all of this," I complain, pushing open the door. Pffft, I say, closing the door again because I can't get out.

I want to go home. Horse Mouth has been staring at me for a while. She says nothing. She seems to be wondering whether I've gone crazy. She grabs her joint from the ashtray, now extinguished, and says, relighting it, "I'll finish this and we'll go back."

We arrive in the neighborhood. She stops at the *tabac*,* enters, comes back out again with a blue plastic bag which she places on her knees, and we leave.

We arrive at my place. She turns off the engine but we don't speak. I have nothing to say anyway. She picks up the gift at my feet, jostling my cane a bit. She sits back up and hands it to me along with an enormous pair of blue scissors which she takes out of the bag of the same color.

"If it still won't open, throw this fucking package out the window for me."

I take the package and I can't help but let a smile creep over my lips. She smiles back and says to me, "Take care of yourself."

And she adds as I lean out of the door to leave:

"And if you need something, anything at all, call me."

I make a gesture with my hand half to say good-bye and half to signal that I heard her. I close the door and start the climb back to my room all over again.

I run into Samira on the first floor. She grabs my arm and as we climb the steps she asks me, "What is that?" while nodding at the package.

"A girl gave it to me. You don't know her."

I have no lie to offer up to her. And anyway, I don't care. It's stupid not to talk about it with Samira. As if I were dealing with matters of state. Why should I, with my pathetic life, insist on lying over nothing?

"I'll tell you once we're up there," I answer, leaning against her even more.

We're in my room. As soon as we entered, I threw myself onto the mattress and Samira gave me a pill.

"So, who is she?" she asks, trying to open the package with her fingers.

"Grab the bottle that's in the armoire."

Since I've been sick, I keep a small stash of wine in the house. I buy bottles in pairs. Samira looks at me, raising an eyebrow. I'm sure she's wondering whether I'm trying to kill time to make her forget her question.

She puts down the package and gets up. She brings back the bottle and pours us each a glass. I take a sip and since the glass is small, I empty it in one gulp. It feels good.

"So, who is she?" she repeats, grabbing the scissors to cut the ribbon.

I told Samira about Horse Mouth without going into too many details. While I was telling her about Hamid, the day we met in the shed and about the film, Samira kept quiet, the gift between her hands. She wasn't looking at me but I could tell she wasn't very happy. Her lips twisted in one direction, then the other.

Now, with all that's happened, I don't even know anymore why I didn't tell her about it. But what exactly would I have told her? That I met a girl who asked me to tell her stories to help her with a film? Do I look like I have a face for movies?

It's not that I didn't trust Samira, it's just that I didn't know she would be the one standing at my side.

I didn't know that she would be the one to sell my two bracelets, my necklace, my scarves to pay my rent, when I had Houcine, the hospital, and all the shit weighing on my shoulders.

I didn't know that she would cook for me, that she would do my laundry, that she would come to see me every day.

And when I had nothing left to sell, how could I have known that she would call Chaïba to borrow money from him and that she would offer for me to live with her if I needed?

How could I have known that she would be this good of a friend? I don't think even she knew it.

And now that I've finished telling her, she's frowning about the Horse.

In case she doesn't know, I've already got a mother who watches over me and sulks. I don't have room for a second. If she's not happy, she can go fuck herself.

"Yeah, well, what I think," she says, handing me the contents of the package, "is that there's no film, no nothing. That girl, she's a freak who has her sights set on you and that's it."

And she adds, "If you had told me, we could at least have really gotten something out of it, more than these trinkets."

I look at the gift. It's a gray scarf, with pink, yellow, and green flowers, very delicate. Silver edges. Next to it, there's an enormous barrette in the shape of a flower. And there's a bag. Gray, with just one flower on the side. Pink. Very chic.

I take them. I don't answer her. Samira's nonsense has nothing to do with this gift. I think she's jealous, that's all.

"Anyway, I'm done with her. I won't see her again after today," I say, pouring myself another glass.

February

MONDAY THE 7TH

Horse Mouth called me several times since the other day, I didn't answer. When I make a decision, I don't go back on it.

I'm lying in front of the television, under two sheets. I just got back from the baths. I took off my djellaba and put on my new robe. It's green and soft as a lamb. I wrapped my head in one of those turban towels that look like hats. I have the new kind that fastens with Velcro.

It's incredibly cold. I light a cigarette and pour myself a small glass. It must be seven or eight at night, I don't know. I feel good. And my leg is better. It still hurts me from time to time but it's a lot better.

I've been resting a lot lately, actually. I've been watching TV, not eating a lot, sleeping. And I've stopped trying to be a hero. Because even in films, when the heroine is sick, she rests in bed.

And on top of all that, I decided to stop worrying about other people. I care so little that even when my husband called me to yell because I hadn't sent him any money since the accident, I let him shout his head off without yelling back. He can climb out of the receiver if he feels like it.

You know what he did the day when I told him I was hit by a motorcycle? Nothing. He went quiet, he muttered a quick "May God heal you" and hung up. I'm sure he was thinking of only one thing: the money I send him every month. Asking himself whether or not the faucet would run dry.

So now he can fuck off.

I take a long drag of my cigarette.

Since seeing her at the hospital, I haven't called Mouy. I can't. The only contact I still have with her is the money orders I send for my daughter.

And for almost two weeks now, none of the girls have stayed with me for more than five minutes. None. They can all fuck off! Them and their worthless visits.

Samira is the only one who's continued to come every day.

"Get up, there's someone here to see you."

Fuck, she's relentless! Samira enters and gestures for someone to come in.

Horse Mouth is behind her. What the hell are they doing together?

"Salaam alaykoum," says Horse Mouth, walking toward me and extending her hand.

"Salaam," I answer sitting up and glancing around me to see what state my room is in. "Welcome."

To tell the truth, I don't know whether to smile at her or not. I didn't want to see her again, but now that she's here, I can't remember why.

"Is that how you welcome guests?" Samira says to me.

And she shows Horse Mouth the other mattress for her to sit on.

Since I've been sick, Samira has made herself at home here.

She mills about, goes to get a glass, sits next to me, jostling me a bit, and takes the bottle of wine to serve her.

Samira's smile takes up as much space as her ass on the mattress.

"You're dying to know what we're doing together, aren't you?"

And she laughs, shaking her head and bouncing her bangs. She's just had her hair done. Normally I like her hair quite a bit but now, she looks like a soccer player. Like that guy Hadji. Short bangs in front and long hair in the back. He has dark hair at the top and light hair at the bottom too. She looks ridiculous. She turns to Horse Mouth. "I told you she'd look like an ass when she saw us together. So, will you explain now?"

Horse Mouth laughs. She takes a cigarette, lights it and explains to me, after taking a drag: "Since I couldn't reach you, I went to the market to see if you were there. I've been going there for several days wondering whether I'd see you or not."

Horse Mouth puts out her cigarette in the glass I use as an ashtray and says, "Since I really needed to talk to you before this Friday, I went to the market today. And I waited for Samira to be alone to speak to her."

I don't bother to ask how she recognized her.

I remember pointing out Samira to her at the market one day while we were driving in the car. Samira cuts her off. "It doesn't matter how we met."

And turning to Horse Mouth, she adds, "Go on, tell her why you're here."

Horse Mouth turns toward me. "Since I came back, I've been working on quite on a few things, but mostly I've been searching for actors. And now I have the cast for all the roles except the heroine."

She continues, "And I'd like for you to do some tests in front of a camera for me. Because the more girls they send me, the more I imagine you in the role instead. I'm sure you'd be great on-screen and that you'd play the role better than anyone else."

I'm stunned. It's like someone just slapped me. Or threw a bucket of water over my head. Whaaaaa! What is she talking about?

Horse Mouth continues. "I can do the screen tests with you, it's easy. We give you some lines, you learn them, you say them in front of the camera, and that's it."

"So, what do you think? Didn't I do a good job bringing her here?" Samira asks, clicking her tongue against the roof of her mouth and throwing me a big wink.

THURSDAY THE 10TH

We're in the taxi, Samira and I, driving to Jus de Bordeaux, the dairy not far from the medina heading toward Boulevard Zerktouni. If you're hungry after a night out, there's nothing better to fill the void. They make you anything you want. But now, I'm not hungry, even though I didn't eat anything this morning.

I have a meeting with Horse Mouth in an office where they'll film me. Samira won't stop cracking jokes. She hasn't shut up since we left the house.

"Do you have diarrhea of the mouth?" I say.

"Are you jealous because you're constipated?" she fires back.

"We're actresses. We're on our way to act in a new film today," she says to the driver, forcing her way into the casting.

"Mmm," mutters the driver, eyeing us in the rearview.

I catch his look in the mirror. Asshole! You don't think we've got the faces to act in films? I don't have time to respond, and it's for the best.

"It's right up here," I say, pointing to the sidewalk for him to stop.

There's a Méditel office on the right. Horse Mouth told me to let her know when we got there. I call her phone and we wait in front of the office. The window is so shiny that we can see ourselves in it like a mirror. We're looking sharp.

I have on my black djellaba, the nice one, not the one I wear for my quick errands. And my hair is loose. Simple but classy. Samira has on her satin leopard-print djellaba, and her hair is pinned up with a big gold barrette she just bought. Her bangs have grown out a bit and look better now.

We look good. Now we just have to see if I can manage to recite these shitty lines. Horse Mouth gave me a page to memorize. And even though she said it's not a problem if I can't memorize it, I practiced, practiced, practiced the text until I had it all in my head. But we'll see how long it'll stay there.

Horse Mouth is crossing the street. And she has her mane up in a ponytail again, like the other day. My stomach hurts. I should have eaten something before I left.

"Salaam," she says.

And she greets Samira too: "I'm glad you came."

Samira's lips spread to her ears. She's so happy, the wretched thing. We head down a small side street that intersects the avenue and we arrive in front of a building on the right. It looks like a normal building. Horse Mouth, without stopping, points at a plaque.

"It's here."

We pass in front of it rapidly and I don't have the time to read what's written on it because it's in French. But I have time to see the design: it's a jumping blue horse with stars circling behind it. I elbow Samira in the stomach, showing her the plaque as Horse Mouth passes in front of it, as if she were reflected in a mirror. Samira puts a finger in front of her mouth to tell me to keep quiet but she's holding back a laugh too.

"It's on the sixth floor," says Horse Mouth, leading us to the elevator.

We're packed in like sardines. Under that white light, I can see Samira's blackheads. The elevator stops at an open apartment. We pass in front of a desk where there's a woman seated in front of a computer, behind a counter. We can hardly see her. She doesn't lift her eyes when we pass and she doesn't greet us. We continue down a hallway.

To our left are several closed doors and an area that looks like a kitchen where we see an old woman. I think she's preparing some tea.

Samira and I walk side by side. We bump into each other because the hallway is narrow and we're looking around us. Everything is yellow here. The walls, the tiles on the floor. Everything.

Horse Mouth walks quickly. We haven't seen anybody else apart from the cleaning lady and the mute sitting at the entrance.

The hallway ends in a room, which we enter. Inside is a woman sitting behind a desk no longer than my forearm. She has a ton of photos and papers in front of her. She lifts her head toward us and stands up, extending her hand.

"Salaam. Jmiaa?"

Samira gestures in my direction to show that I'm Jmiaa. I reach out my hand. She says, "Lamia. I'm the casting director. I'm the one who meets with the actors for the film."

"Salaam," I answer, extending my hand.

She motions to the room next door, allowing me to enter ahead of her.

I think I've forgotten my lines.

The walls are white. There's a camera in the middle and three chairs. That's all. It looks like a hospital.

I've forgotten my lines, I'm sure of it.

Behind the chairs, there's a large window with a balcony that overlooks the building opposite. Horse Mouth and Samira follow us.

"Okay, we're going to start off nice and easy. For now, we won't use the text I gave you," explains Horse Mouth. "First, you'll stand here, you'll look at the camera. You'll say your last name, your first name, your age, turn to the right, turn to the left, and then look right at the camera and smile. Stand here."

Horse Mouth shows me a spot not far from the wall. She sits in a chair that she grabs from the corner of the room, and the girl named Lamia stands next to the camera.

"My real name, my real age, right?" I specify, running my hand through my hair to flatten it.

She says yes. Easy. "Bent Larbi Jmiaa, thirty-five years old."

And I turn right and left and straight ahead. I think I did okay.

Horse Mouth gets up, she walks toward me and says, "Now, we're going to do a simple scene. You'll pretend you've just received a call from your mother and you can't hear her. You're busy walking in the street, your phone rings and it's your mother. But you can't really hear what she's saying."

"And the text that I memorized?"

"Forget about the text for now."

Today is my lucky day.

"So you're walking, the telephone rings and it's your mother, okay?"

"Mouy?" I repeat, behind her.

"Yes, your mother?!" she responds, as if she were asking me a question.

I have no desire to talk to Mouy. Not even if it's pretend.

"You know what, pretend you're talking to your sister," continues Horse Mouth. "Even if you don't have one. Or like you're talking to Samira, but you can't hear her."

I told you I got lucky today.

"Okay," I answer. "And what do I say to her?"

"Whatever you want. Say what you would in real life."

And she adds: "Okay, let's start?"

With no text to memorize, this will be easy. I just pose in front of the camera and that's all.

Horse Mouth signals to me with her hand that I can start talking. A red button lights up on the side of the camera.

"Hello, Samira? Where are you?" I say, annunciating well and looking straight at the camera.

I flash an impeccable smile, I tuck my bag under my shoulder and continue. "No, I can't talk to you right now. Later."

I walk a bit to the right, as if I were in the street. "No, I can't really hear you. There's too much noise."

I put my finger in the other ear and look toward the sky. I make sure my little finger is raised, separated from the others. They do that in films when there's a girl from a well-to-do family and she's talking on the phone. Half turn!

Horse Mouth is chewing her hair. Samira suppresses a laugh. What does that asshole have to giggle about? I'll deal with her later.

I wait a bit, as if someone were answering me on the other end of the telephone. "No, later. I can't talk to you right now," I continue, looking at the camera and posing appropriately.

Samira is bothering me. All I can see now is her and her smile. She's sitting with her butt cheeks spilling over the sides of the chair, her ankles crossed beneath her djellaba, and she's hiding her crooked teeth with her big pudgy hammam-masseuse fingers. What a jackass!

Horse Mouth is sitting in silence. She's looking at me.

I have to pay attention to my hands. I have a tendency to use them a bit too much when I speak. "Hello, Samira? Yes, I can hear you. I'm a bit busy right now. Can I call you back later when I'm free?"

"Pffft!"

That bitch Samira!

"What the fuck are you laughing about?" I ask her, turning to look at her and flinging my right hand off to the side. I want to slap her.

"Oh, fuck off. You've never talked to me like that!"

And she imitates me acting overly ingratiating, like a whore, hand in her ear as if she were holding a phone: "Hello, Samira? No, I can't talk to you right now. I'm busy."

She speaks softly, drawing out each word and pouting her dick-sucking lips as if there were a guy holding her from behind. Asshole!

I yell, "What are you bitching about? And who do you think you are, opening your big mouth?"

I'll show her, talking to me like that. I walk toward her. She gets up too. I'm standing firm on my legs. She is too, but if she thinks she's going to scare me, she's wrong. If she says another word, I'll wreck her face.

"Incredible! That's exactly what we need." Horse Mouth jumps up, placing one hand on my chest and the other on Samira's. Where did she come from? She's suddenly between us and turns toward the girl who's working the camera.

"Play that back for me."

And to me she says, "That's exactly how you should do it. Launch into it without thinking. You see what you did with Samira just now? That's what you have to do."

And she turns toward Samira, laughing, "It's a good thing you came."

What does she mean, that's how I have to do it? What does that cunt want? For me and Samira to argue? That's what she wants?

Horse Mouth is behind the camera. She's watching on a small screen, like a television, that's popped out of the side of the camera.

"Come and see," she says, waving me and Samira over.

On the screen, Samira and I are about to break into a fight. We look like witches and there's nothing all that unusual about the spectacle. We shout.

"You see, it's incredible! Look."

Incredible? How is that incredible? Samira is standing, I'm opposite her. Our fists on our hips. And I have a tuft of hair coming out of my head like an antenna.

"Are you crazy?" I say to Horse Mouth. "You think you're going to film me like that? Are you trying to make a fool of me?"

And I say to Samira, laughing, "This chick is really crazy."

"All right, you know what? Let's go for a cigarette," says Horse Mouth, opening the door to the outside.

*W*e're on the balcony. If they hadn't insisted, I would have taken off just now. She wants to film me with my hair sticking straight up, is she crazy?

"Here."

The old woman who was in the kitchen holds out a tray with cups of tea for me to take. Her face is all wrinkled, and she's wearing a white blouse.

I take a cup.

I remain standing. There are only three tiny chairs on the balcony. You can't fit half your thigh on them they're so small. And they're low too.

So I remain standing. Horse Mouth takes a cup and says to the old woman, bowing as if she were greeting the king, "God bless you, Mouy Mina."

The woman smiles, mouth gaping. A toothless king. And she goes back inside.

"It has to be like real life. It's a film, but it has to be like real life. For people to believe it. For them to think it really happened."

"You want to make a fool of me? You want me to be on the television looking like that? That's not okay."

Samira agrees with me. She says nothing but she agrees, it's obvious. At least there's someone here who understands.

"Don't worry, there won't be any scenes like that in the film. And there won't be a scene where you look ugly or where you don't like how you look," Horse Mouth responds. "What I wanted to say earlier, when you were talking to Samira, is that it was real. On the camera, it was real and that was obvious, do you understand what I'm trying to say?"

"Of course it was real. I almost ripped out her hair."

Samira is silent. She's already finished her cigarette and she has her arms crossed in front of her chest.

"What I mean to say is that it was true. What happens on the screen when you're yourself is something special. Listen, there are loads of actresses. There are good ones, and there are average ones. There are pretty ones, ugly ones, fat ones, you get the idea, there are loads of actresses. And each one, when she's chosen for a film, is hired either because the director wants to film her and not someone else, or because she has something that the others don't. You, you're both. I want you to act in my film. You have a power that radiates from you that...that fills the room. That fills the screen."

Samira nods her head from top to bottom. She thinks I should do it.

"There will be makeup, they'll dress you. It'll be a good thing, you'll see. Anyway, I told you, the film won't be shown in Morocco. It'll only be shown abroad, where people understand that it's a film and that you have to play the role the way things happen in real life."

She stops talking and we keep puffing on our cigarettes. There are clouds starting to cover the sky. We stay like that for a little while. I put out my cigarette in the ashtray on the ground and I start walking back into the room. "Come on, let's go."

I open my bag. The other three look at me. I take out my mirror and my lipstick, I put it on, taking my time. I fix my hair. I walk toward the center of the room and I say, glancing over my shoulder, "What are you waiting for? An official invitation?"

Lamia gets behind the camera, Horse Mouth sits to the side and Samira plops down like a dope on the chair in the back.

I begin. "Hello, Samira? Listen, I can't talk to you right now," I yell, plugging my ear where there's no phone.

Frowning, standing at a slant, my right side angled toward the camera, I add, "I'll call you back later! Huh? I'll call you back later. Why? I can't hear you. Hello? Pffft."

I try to hear Samira's response in the telephone but the fucking signal is shitty. I continue, "I told you I'll call you back later. Yeah, yeah, that's right. Go on, go fuck yourself. Bye."

And I hang up. I look at Horse Mouth. All her teeth are showing. I think I've done a good job. "Incredible!" she says. "That was very good. Let's do a final test with the real script."

MONDAY THE 28TH

Truly, my luck has been strange recently. If someone is watching over me from the beyond, I have no idea who it might be.

In Casablanca and in all of Morocco, chaos broke out when that Tunisian guy poured gasoline over his head. It's been two Sundays since then and downtown still hasn't emptied. Everyone who's in want of something, everyone who has nothing to put in their mouths, everyone who's at war with their wives, everyone who isn't happy with their circumcision, they've all taken to the street. Everyone has their own demand.

It gets on my nerves. There's no more order around here. When I saw them all arrive, I thought maybe there'd be more opportunities for work or something like that. But in reality, there's no work, no nothing. Nothing but hassles, like always.

Yesterday was Sunday, I was calmly waiting in the street. A little bit past the market, on that road that intersects the avenue. That way, I could take care of my business and see what was happening with the protesters at the same time.

When I saw the cop, or maybe it was a Cimi,* I retreated a little so he wouldn't bother me. With all this mess around them right now, they're quicker to fly off the handle. And I have no desire to be hit with a stray bludgeon since I've only been back out here for the last few days.

Anyway, I was standing on the street and a group of young guys approached me. I don't like it when young people hang out in packs. They don't belong to any religion or other group. You have to be on the lookout with them because you never know what might happen.

The other night, Samira could have been slashed to pieces. There were three kids who came to see her. She went up with one and when he finished, he told her that his friend downstairs had the money. That bothered Samira, but she went down with him anyway. Her plan was to take the money and send the other two on their way, even if they wanted to do something with her. Once they were downstairs, they refused to pay. So she said to the one who had come up, looking him straight in the eyes, "Cough it up, you nasty kid. Cough it up or I'll make you regret it, you'll bring shame to your entire family."

"Oh yeah? And who's around to hear you at this hour, you dirty whore," he answered, looking left and right in the street.

There was only Samira and his two friends around. Samira got mad and started to say, at first softly and then, faced with his silence, louder and louder, "Cough it up, cough it up, cough it up."

On the fifth or sixth time, she let loose her siren song. And normally, those little brats get scared when you start to yell. But that night those parasites didn't budge and the one who had gone up with her said in her face, with a vicious smile, "Remember what I did to you up there? Well, I'll do it again down here. Over there, under the porch. And this time, my friends will join in," he added, pointing at the door of the building next to the restaurant that had just opened, starting to undo his zipper.

Before he could finish his sentence, he realized that Samira was running toward our building, yelling at everything she could. It must have been one in the morning. The three others followed her, also yelling: "Dirty whore, we're going to catch you and fuck up your face."

Samira was holding her djellaba above her waist with both hands, she abandoned her sandals in the street and took off in a sprint like she hadn't done in a long time, she said. It wasn't until she'd arrived at the bottom of the building, where the night guard was, that she turned around to insult them and throw rocks in their faces. They took off back where they had come from. And Samira went upstairs, her hair disheveled. She woke me up and we finished my bottle while she called them all the names she could think of, those sons of bitches. If they had caught her... It's best not to think about it.

Anyway, yesterday when those kids approached, like an idiot I hung around the small street to the left, just to see if they were going to follow me or not. They followed me. I sped up to keep them at a distance. The street curves, and I knew that at the end there was the avenue full of people. But from where I was, I couldn't see it. That street is peculiar: you're walking along on the sidewalk and then suddenly the road passes under a building. It's like a tunnel. And when I reached the bend, I saw that the end of the street was blocked by barriers. I quickly turned around, thinking that in any event it was the middle of the day and those young people might try to pull something but it wouldn't go very far. One of them looked at me and said. "Hey, you, come over here. Where are you going?"

I turned toward them and got a better look. This wasn't a pack of dogs. They were clean and well dressed. Students, surely. But that doesn't mean they were smiling and welcoming. They looked at me as if they were staring at a stinking pile of shit, excuse my language. I didn't respond and continued on my way. They crossed the street so that they were right in front of me. They surrounded me. There were four of them. A violet djellaba passed at the end of the street. I waved to her but she took off. When I saw that I was cornered, I softened, thinking that I would butter them up. I put my hands on my hips and angled my chest toward them, saying, "Which of you would like a taste of something sweet?"

They looked at each other, laughing, and all at the same time, they said:

"Whore!"

"We'll give you a lesson you won't forget."

"That'll teach you to walk through these streets wiggling your behind."

"...perverting the people..."

"...devil..."

"...right path..."

After a moment, I could only hear fragments of what they were saying because they were all talking at the same time. I was about to start insulting them and push one so I could get away when I heard a booming voice behind them say, "What are you doing? We came here to protest, not to engage in things like this."

They all jumped and turned toward the man. He must have been fifty years old. He was wearing gray suit pants and a white shirt. The first thing I noticed was that it was very clean. His hair was half-black, half-gray, and he had a small, well-groomed beard, dark black. He didn't turn his head toward me for a second. His face didn't express anything in particular. As soon as he spoke, the man turned his back to us and started to walk away. He didn't need to say anything more for the dogs to tuck their tails between their legs and follow him. I don't know if he was their boss or their imam or what. I don't know how those Islamic organizations function.

Behind them, the violet djellaba I had seen run past earlier brought up the rear. She was the one who had called the older man. When my gaze met hers, the woman lowered her eyes.

It was Halima. Halima who had lived with me in my room.

I didn't have time to say anything to her. Because all of this happened in a flash. In any event, there was nothing to say. The truth is that when I saw her, I felt a bit uncomfortable. But who knows, maybe she has no idea that I was the one who told Houcine to kick her out.

And besides, everyone has their own destiny. I'm starting to believe in all that bullshit. Who would have thought, for example, that I would act in a film? Who would have thought that on top of it, I would play the most important role and be paid well for it? Who? No one.

Maybe there are things that happen in life for no reason. Or maybe everything that happens is already foreseen, planned, outlined, all of it. Like in a film.

March

The day is over and I still haven't had a drop to drink. I only took some of those pills that knock me out and now I'm sitting alone in my room.

I have the script in front of me.

When the guy who works with Horse Mouth gave it to me—about ten days ago—he explained to me that I have to learn my part, meaning all the places where "Hasna" is written. And you know how many times Hasna is written in this script? One or two thousand times. I have no idea how I'm going to memorize all of this.

But I've had no problem learning the story, it's easy. It's like a film. You simply follow it.

In the story, my name is Hasna. I work on the street and I have a boyfriend. His name is Brahim.

I've never been married and I don't have children. I don't speak to my parents anymore, nor to my family. I don't have any girlfriends, I have no one. And basically I live on the street. The truth is that I'm in deep shit.

The guy, my boyfriend, he's a real son of a bitch! You can't imagine what a son of a bitch he is. He and I, we decide to carry out a heist together in a jewelry store—thinking that will get us out of our shit. I give him the jeweler's schedule, he's an old fogey, his shop is on the street where I work. I describe his routine to my boyfriend, and he does the robbery. That idiot, once he's pulled it off, he grabs all the necklaces, all the bracelets, all the watch chains, and he takes off, leaving me like an asshole on the sidewalk. Then, lots of things happen. With the police, the neighbors... It's an unbelievable mess. There are investigators who come and interrogate people. I'm interrogated too, but they don't know I'm a part of the heist. And after that, other things happen too: I meet another guy, named Mouad, who likes me, one of my clients commits suicide, I'm assaulted. That's another horrendous mess.

Next, Mouad and I, we get together and go off looking for the bastard. We're lucky because—serves the guy right—we find him dead in the room where he was hiding out. And since he didn't tell anyone where he was, no one else found him first. So we take all the gold and get out of there. You see us take off in a car on a road where there's no one else, just us two, there's music playing, a bag full of gold on my knees, and we're happy. But that's still not the end.

We stop at a gas station near the Algerian border, I get out to piss and when I come back, the idiot's taken off, leaving me in the middle of nowhere. And that's it, that's the end of the film.

If you want my opinion, I think that part's horrible, and if I'd written the script, I would have stopped earlier, when we were in the car. But that cunt Horse Mouth didn't want it that way, so that's the story.

The guy who gave it to me told me that from now on, I have to keep this script with me at all times. I have to spend all my free time reading it. When I'm eating, when I'm waiting somewhere, when I'm in the bathroom, all the time, until it's coming out of my ears. As if I'd eaten too much, and instead of food bursting out of me, it's the script.

And that's what I do. Whenever I can, I take the script and I read it. I read, I read, I read. All the time. At first, it was a bit difficult because I hadn't read anything since the end of elementary school apart from signs, but now, it's fine. It's come back.

When I'm not reading, I'm going over it in my head. I've cut back my work in the streets to a minimum, just enough to pay the people I owe.

Except for my husband, because I think I've managed to get rid of him for now. I haven't told him that I've started working again. Every time he called, I told him I couldn't, that I was in a bad state. And every time, I stopped at the description of my shitty situation just before attracting the attention of the evil eye. You never know. Even better: the last time I spoke to him, I told him that *he* had to send *me* money to help me pay for the medications and that he had to send money to Mouy for his daughter. Since that day, he hasn't called back. I can rest easy for the moment.

You know, I'm not going to tell anyone else that I'm acting in a film. Otherwise they're all going to start coming up with pipe dreams. As if we're going to make billions. Well, honestly, what I'm going to make isn't half bad. I'm not going to be as rich as the king, but I've done well for myself.

They called me one morning, I had just woken up. It was a guy I'd never heard of. He told me that he was calling on behalf of the film production company. He wanted me to come see him in the afternoon, at the same place where I went to do the screen test. I said okay, but since I didn't know who this pimp was, I called Horse Mouth first. It turned out that she knew him. She knew that he was calling me to talk about money. To tell me how much I would be paid for the film.

I got dressed, I put myself together, and I took off. Alone. I didn't bring Samira with me. I saw that she was busy so I didn't ask her to come. And to tell the truth, it was better that way.

When I arrived, the mute at the entrance had me go into one of those rooms that was closed the first time. It was also yellow, like the hallway. There was a man sitting inside. I entered and I remained standing until he told me to sit. He was wearing glasses. He was tall. And rather skinny. He had a serious air about him, like a school principal. He stressed me out. I sat down and I almost didn't speak. He told me that he was going to give me two million and that he was preparing the contract. And then I left. That was it. I didn't have time to understand what was happening, and then it was already over.

When I told Horse Mouth how much they had offered me, she made a funny face and when I pushed to find out why she was making that expression, I understood that I should have been paid more. Because as soon as we start filming, they're going to put me up at a hotel and I won't be able to work anymore. From now until then, I can. But as soon as we start filming, I'll have to stop.

So we talked, we made an agreement about the amount that I would ask for, and I called the guy back to negotiate. I was relentless. I asked for five million. In the end, we both compromised and met in the middle. And that's how I raised the amount to three and a half million, and I got to work.

I would never have thought that I could kick so much ass. I have no idea how this all happened to me. I'm not saying the script entered into my head by magic. Not at all, far from it. I've been working my ass off. Whenever I'm not at the market, I devour the script. I even have a whole system for practicing.

The first thing I did, since it's not practical to carry such a big notebook under my arm all the time, is that I tore out all the pages. It's easier to walk with sheets of paper than with a notebook. And most importantly, it saves me from embarrassment. The other day, I don't know what came over me, but I went out with the entire notebook. That's all anyone saw. The entire neighborhood made fun of me: "Studying for your anatomy class?" "You don't think you have enough padding on your behind to cushion your seat?" "Did you get a job at the moqataa*?"

Let them laugh, with their big flapping mouths. Later, we'll see who's laughing. While I'm making my money, they'll be swallowing flies.

Here at the house, I piled up all the sheets of paper. They're all neatly arranged. When I go out to bring someone up, I quickly gather them into one big pile that I stash under the table. And I cover it all with a plastic tablecloth that hangs to the ground.

And if I want to practice while I'm in the street, I just take out the relevant sheet. When I forget the line, I quickly unfold the piece of paper, I read it, and I put it back in its place, in my bra. No one has noticed anything yet.

I'm also at home most of the time. Since I've started working on the film, I've been locking the door to my room to have peace and quiet. I only go out when I need to go out. And as soon as I've made my keep for the day, I come back home to relax and mind my own business.

"Open sesame!"

Samira whispers behind the door, "Open sesame, motherfucker, open this door, if you would be so kind."

As soon as she has a free moment, she comes to see me and we rehearse together. She takes the script and concentrates deeply to decipher it all, and she plays the other characters. I say Hasna's lines that I've memorized. When I forget a word or a sentence or what comes next, Samira tells me.

I promised her that I would bring her with me to the shoot one day. They announced that it would start at the beginning of April. And that it would last a little more than a month. Five weeks.

I open the door and a gust of cold air enters the room. Time to warm up with a drink.

"So, where were we?" Samira asks, gesturing dramatically with her arm.

"Come in, we'll have a glass and we'll remember," I answer.

She enters and sits down. "So, how did it go? Were you there today?"

"Sit down first," I say to her, taking out the bottle I still keep in the cabinet.

I did tests today. At the same place again. I borrowed a djellaba from Samira to change things up a bit and I put on the scarf that Chaïba gave me when I was sick. Back when we still spoke. Since then, I've decided to stop seeing that piece of shit. You remember how that moron went off with Hajar to piss me off when I didn't answer his call? And remember how when I was sick, he gave Samira some money for me?

When he helped me, I let go of what happened with Hajar. I told myself that everyone makes mistakes and does stupid things. And since on top of it that bitch never misses an opportunity to piss me off, I told myself that she must have gotten him worked up on a night when he was good and drunk. And I forgave him.

I was going to call him to meet up but I didn't have the chance. Ten days ago, I happened to run into him at Pommercy. With that whore Hajar again. And then Samira told me that she had run into them together twice. And that bitch, every time she saw Samira, bared all her teeth.

I'm sure she wriggles her ass in front of Chaïba just so that Samira will come and tell me. I know perfectly well what she's up to, that little slut. She flirts with men by giving them bitch-in-heat eyes. And she walks with her butt cheeks sticking out, like a goose. I'd like to think that each night Bouchaïb left with her, she's the one who came onto him. But when did he get so stupid? Did he eat the brain of a hyena? Humiliating me like that. Taking off with that worthless whore. In front of everyone. Leaving with her when he knows that she and I are like cat and mouse! No, that's not cool.

Anyway, I don't even know anymore how much I've told you or where we were in my story. Oh yes! I was telling you that I went to the office to try on clothes.

When I arrived, it was the first time I had seen so many people there. They were milling about everywhere and I felt lost. Our elders say, "If you're lost, hang on to the ground." That's what I did. I sat down on one of those three chairs lined up in the entrance.

The mute wasn't in her usual place and I waited for someone to come. Loads of people passed by me. Someone entered, others left. There were all kinds of people: blond, black, latte colored. There were people speaking in Arabic, others in French, and others who spoke in a language that sounded like Berber but which wasn't Berber. I think it was Dutch. And everyone was busy.

Eventually, a girl came to ask me if I needed help.

I told her I was there to try on clothes. "Okay, who is it for?"

I looked at her. I didn't understand her stupid question. What does she mean, who is it for? It's for me. So I responded, "Jmiaa."

She gave me an idiotic look. I figured she must have been a bit stupid, so I took out my ID. She grabbed it but she didn't even glance at it. She said to me, handing it back, "And it's for what role?"

"I'm Hasna. I'm playing the role of the girl, the one who's tricked in the end by that asshole Mouad."

Immediately, she understood. She bared her teeth in a smile and said, "Ah! Salaam, my name is Yasmine."

And then she added, "Come with me."

And she started to walk down the hallway until we arrived in front of a door that she pushed open. She called out, speaking to two women who were sitting in the room, "For Hasna."

She told me that they'd take care of me. And she left.

The room was huge. It was a living room but inside there was no mattress, no table, no nothing. There were only clothes on racks. And to the side, standing against a wall with a big window, was a long table covered in a heap of fabric, with scissors, pins, sewing tools. There were two women. A blonde, foreign, a giant with short hair, a bit of a mess. And a young woman, Moroccan, standing opposite her.

The blonde must have been fifty years old. She said her name was Ludmilla. I remember her name—even though it's a bit unusual—because there was a Ludmilla in a Mexican soap opera I watched a long time ago.

The young woman next to her had curly black hair. Because she was Moroccan, her name was Lamia. She was wearing jeans. She seemed normal. They both smiled and set down their fabric. They had me try on three typical djellabas. There was a black one, a green one, and a red one with yellow flowers on it. It didn't take long. The djellabas were exactly my size. It's what happened next that scared the shit out of me.

"Here," I say to Samira, "see if you can understand this."

And I hand her a pile of papers they had given me after the fitting. When I went there, I didn't know that I would have to see anyone other than the seamstresses. When I finished trying on the last djellaba, the Moroccan woman said, "Come with me, they want to see you in production."

We walked until we arrived in another office I hadn't been in before. Inside was Yasmine from earlier. And that's when things started to get complicated. Yasmine stood next to me and took out a pile of papers arranged in a pink folder. She pulled them out one after another, placing them on the table in front of me as she showed them to me and explained what was written on each one. Honestly? I understood nothing.

There were a dozen papers, each one filled with charts, full of colors. Every color under the sun. And on each sheet were thirty or forty lines, something like that. And Yasmine said that in there I would find the schedule, day by day, the location where they were going to film, the actors, the sets, the dialogues we had to learn. It was written in French. I just stood there, I didn't know what to do.

I understood only one thing: the yellow squares with the number 2, those are the days when I film. That's the only thing I took away from all of that crap.

But I didn't tell her that. Soon I was no longer paying attention to what she was saying, but I was nodding yes all the same. I let her talk until she was finished. I didn't stop her. When she was done, I told her it was all fine and—quickly—before she could start another sentence, I told her to please excuse me, but I had to go to see my paternal aunt who was sick. And I took off.

I'm reassured: Samira doesn't understand a thing either.

"So?" I ask her on the off chance, lighting a cigarette.

"What is this crap?"

I laugh and answer, "No clue."

"Why don't you have the Horse explain it to you?" she asks, turning to face me.

"That's what I was thinking."

I don't know how I'm going to manage all of this. I swear, I don't know how I'm going to manage all of this.

April

MONDAY THE 11TH

Today's the day, we're about to start filming. Here they say *tournage*, in French.

We're sitting, Horse Mouth and I, at the entrance of a hotel called the Hotel d'Anfa. It's not very far from downtown, in Maârif, next to Twin.* We'll live here until the end of filming.

It's early. Not even nine in the morning and we've already had breakfast. We're dressed, showered. My feet move on their own. I can't sit still. We're waiting for the car that will bring us to the set. Since it's the first day, we're going together. After today I'll go alone, she told me. They'll send a car with a driver. He'll bring me to the set every day. And every night when I'm finished, no matter how late, he'll bring me back. Classy, right?

Today, I'm going to film four scenes. Last night, Horse Mouth told me not to worry about how their confusing charts work. Each night, she'll tell me what I need to learn for the next day. At least that's one less thing to worry about.

Horse Mouth and I are sitting on a brown sofa. There's a stranger with us. He has blond hair, glasses, and he's also a giant. Horse Mouth told me his position in the film but I don't remember what it was. Director of something. And to tell the truth, I was a bit distracted. I was busy looking at the decor.

We're in a lobby, and what a lobby! It's like a soccer field. The ceiling goes to the sky and the stairs that lead to the second floor—covered in red carpet with gold embroidery on the sides—are at least six feet wide. The sofas are as big as boats. When you see humans sitting on them, they look like ants.

No matter where we go, horses follow us. There's a huge statue right in the middle of the lobby, made from iron. There's a man sitting on the horse. He's wearing a selham* and a turban and he's holding a rifle. He's going to a fantasia.* Probably to a big moussem.* Horse Mouth doesn't pay attention to it. She doesn't pay attention to anything anyway.

She's too busy with her folders. And eating her hair. Judging by her face, I don't think she's had much sleep. She looks a bit frantic, the poor thing. I am too, if I'm being honest.

But it's not because I'm afraid. It's the lack of sleep. I am a *little* afraid, if I'm honest, but it's mostly because I got a bit carried away last night.

They put me up in a room that's unlike anything you've ever seen in your life.

The way the door opens is already enough to give you a glimpse of what awaits. It opens with a card, like the ones you use to recharge your phone. When the guy who was carrying my bags slid it into the slot, I watched how he did it, discreetly. I memorized the movement in my head and as soon as he left, I reopened the door and practiced until I had mastered the technique.

Then I started to make myself at home.

The room was huge, with a window overlooking the city as if it were a movie screen. And a bed as big as a field. Inside, you could fit me, Samira, and my daughter—and there would still be room for more if you wanted.

But I have to mention two things in particular.

The first is the fridge. Black, small. You wouldn't spend two rials on it. But when you open it, that's another story. Coke, Fanta, orange juice, and bottles of all sorts of things. There's beer, whiskey, vodka, wine. You think of something—anything you want—it's in there.

My other favorite thing, which made me think that these movie people really know how to live, is the bathroom. A bathtub, a shower, towels, soaps, shampoos, body lotion. If you can resist the temptation of it all, there's only one possible conclusion: you love grime.

I didn't think twice.

I went into the bedroom and stripped down to how God made me. Next, I loaded myself up with the contents of the fridge, I went back to the bathroom, and I got the party started!

A sip, a little dip. Another sip. Another dip. And so on.

It reminded me of a guy I brought home one day. He told me stories I had assumed were bullshit. His name was Fettah, I remember him well. He was working as a chauffeur for an Italian guy. One day the Italian brought him into a classy hotel room like this one. In Jdida. The guy had booked a room for himself and a room for the chauffeur. When he saw the price of the room on the door, twenty-six thousand rials, Fettah almost choked. And then he spent half the night awake trying to take advantage of it.

Well, that's exactly what I did yesterday. After that, how do you expect me to be fresh this morning?

We're here. We've arrived at the filming location. It's an old building, constructed during the French occupation, next to the central market.

It's really tall, like the other buildings in the neighborhood. The sun is starting to beat down. It's going to be a hot one today.

"Ready?" Horse Mouth says, getting out of the car and turning toward me.

"One minute, I have to get some nicotine into my lungs," I answer, getting out and lighting a cigarette.

Today, we're shooting scenes in the guy's apartment, Hasna's Brahim. Oh, I didn't tell you, but I've already met him. Guess who he is. I don't know how I didn't mention it before. The day I found out, I didn't know what to do with myself I was so surprised. It's Kaïs Joundy! Do you know who that is? The guy who acted in *Two Men to Kill*. He's such a hunk! Incredible!

Well, to tell the truth, I think he's a bit too skinny for the role. They should have cast someone with more muscles. Like that asshole Chaïba for example. He might be a jerk, but he's huge. Or else someone who looks like Hamid, my husband. With thick hair and deep, black eyes. Eyes you could drown in.

When I said that to Horse Mouth, she replied that he's a good actor and that they would fix him up so that when I saw him, I would change my mind.

I saw him the other day when we were at Horse Mouth's, in a studio that belongs to her aunt in the building next to the parking garage. From her terrace, you can see the market, the park, the square with the pigeons, you can see everything that happens in the neighborhood and all the people you know. I saw that son of a whore Bachir the grocer, the one who rips us off on beer prices, remember him? I sent a gob of spit his way! I was so fast that the other two didn't even see it. Serves him right!

Horse Mouth, Kaïs, and I rehearsed the script several times. Horse Mouth says what happens in the scene, and you do what she says. For example, in something we're going to film today, Brahim hits Hasna because she slept with another man. So she hits him back and they start arguing and hitting each other. To guide you in how you should act out the scene, Horse Mouth says things like "When he hits you and you get mad, think of a moment in your life when you felt the same anger. When you were so angry that if you didn't bite your tongue until it bled, or squeeze your fists tight as hell, you would have buried your fingers in the other person until his intestines popped out of his eyes." Horse Mouth didn't say it like that but I understood. I know what real anger feels like.

When we rehearsed the scene, "Kaïs Brahim" and I, I didn't think about anything. Every time I tried to concentrate, I saw Horse Mouth look at me, I looked at Kaïs, I found it all idiotic and it threw me off. So we'd have to start over. Horse Mouth made us rehearse so many times that it did my head in. Finally, I twisted the brat's wrist because he was starting to piss me off hitting me like that all morning and I threw my script and the bottle of beer right in his face.

"Asshole! It's not like there are no other men left on earth, I don't have to put up with this shit!"

Kaïs felt my wrath. Horse Mouth laughed. And she said that was it, I was ready. Later, we all drank beers together and in the end it was a good night.

I finish my cigarette. Horse Mouth tells me we have to go, and that from now on, Jaafar—a guy who works with her—will take care of me. And that she's going to make sure that everything is ready to go on set. She's just finished her sentence and we're still outside when a badly shaven guy in jeans with hair like a sheep arrives. He has dark-brown skin. Even though it's hot, he's wearing a black leather jacket as shiny as his gel-soaked hair. He's clearly very into himself.

"Salaam, Jmiaa? Come with me?" he says with a nod of the head. And he turns back around.

His ass is squeezed tight in his blue jeans. He's holding a big walkie-talkie in his hand, like the ones the police carry. We enter the building, take the elevator, and go up.

"Here we are. I'll take you to the dressing room."

In the apartment, there are a ton of people. Everyone is busy. The ones who notice us—the others are too busy—vaguely nod their heads to say hello. The playboy walking in front of me responds just as vaguely. We arrive at the dressing room. I see the giant seamstress and the girl who was with her before, Lamia.

"How long will you be?" he asks them, glancing at his watch. It's a quarter to ten.

The Moroccan and the foreigner speak between themselves and the Moroccan girl turns to him and says, "Let's say twenty minutes. 11:05."

"Okay, I'll wait here," he says, indicating the door. He grabs the walkie-talkie crackling in his hand, speaks into it, and walks out.

"How are you?" the blonde asks me.

She spoke in French but she enunciated each word. So that I would understand.

"I'm good, hamdoullah,*" I answer.

"We're going to get you dressed, it'll be quick. And then Jaafar will take you to hair and makeup."

Before I realize what's happening, I'm standing there in my bra and underwear. Fuck, my head is spinning!

From behind the door, I hear the playboy's voice. "All good? Is she ready?"

The Moroccan girl says, "It's only the first day of filming, Jaafar. You're not going to start pestering us with your tight schedule already."

They dress me and open the door. Jaafar, without speaking, signals for me to follow him.

I look in the mirror next to the door. I no longer feel the heat from earlier. The djellaba they put me in is light red. They gave me an orange scarf. Not bad. Also light. They tied it around my neck and picked out some pretty sandals. With a large black band across the front and a sole that looks like cork. Pretty high. They don't slide. The only shitty thing about my outfit is the chipped nail polish on my toes.

Just as I'm about to walk out, Lamia turns to me and says, also in French, "Go on, good luck."

I want to shit myself.

They brought me to the makeup artist and to the hairdresser—both in the same room—and now I'm standing in the middle of the set. There are a ton of people. Horse Mouth told me that we would be filming the scene we practiced in her studio, the one with the beer. How does she expect me to do anything with all this chaos? With all the machines and noise. And all these people speaking but you can't hear anything they're saying. Horse Mouth disappeared once Jafaar brought me to her office after hair and makeup. She said I looked impeccable, and then she ran off. Impeccable my ass. If I wasn't so polite, I would have shown the hairdresser where she could shove her curling iron. She fussed over my head for a full half hour, and you can barely tell the difference from when I walked in.

Fortunately, there's the makeup to salvage the situation. You can't even imagine all the products the girl used. She is gifted, but she's a real bitch. When she finished, since there were nail polishes on the dressing table, I asked her if she had remover, showing her the chipped polish on my hands and feet. She looked at my fingers for a long time, she told me she would ask and she left. You're going to ask? What exactly are you going to ask? You're going to ask if you're going to let me humiliate myself or not? And ask who? Stupid bitch!

The problem is that when she came back, she told me they were going to leave it like that. That it would be better that way. What choice did I have? Grab the bottle and her ponytail by force? When I've only just arrived and don't know anyone here yet? Country whore!

"Go ahead, Jmiaa, let's rehearse so that everyone can learn their role."

Horse Mouth appeared like a she-devil. Suddenly she's right in front of me. We're getting down to business now.

I really have to shit. I wish my ass would leave me in peace!

And you, Jmiaa, it's time to show them what you can do!

All that crap was so tiring. When you think of film actors, you imagine them sitting by a hotel pool, sipping an orange juice. You think it must be so cool. You would never imagine that they spend the whole day rehearsing the same scene endlessly. It's maddening.

Now I'm sitting in the big armchair in my hotel room drinking a beer. But the entire day, I was standing. We went from one scene to another almost without stopping. I don't know how many scenes we filmed.

We worked so much, and I didn't get to take advantage of anything. Not lunch, not the fridge on the terrace. Although they did serve us an incredible lunch. There was everything. A meat tagine with peas and artichokes, a chicken tagine with potatoes, salads of every kind, eggplants, peppers, cucumbers, tomatoes, fruit, Dannon yogurts. And after, on a separate table, there was dessert. It's really a shame I wasn't able to enjoy it.

To tell the truth, they made me dizzy with all their bullshit today. We started with screen tests. If you want to know what exactly they were testing, and what all those guys were doing with their machines, you'd have to ask them. Because I have no idea. All I know is that they told us the scene was just for practice, not the real thing.

I struggled at first. With all the ruckus they were making as we filmed, I couldn't concentrate. At one point, they all started to yell as if they were bidding at a fish auction.

First one guy screams something. Then another guy, who's sitting behind a tiny table as if he were being punished, says something else. Then some nutjob jumps up thrusting a long rod full of hair that looks like the brooms we use to clean the ceiling, right in your face.

And next, the cameraman, followed by Horse Mouth, who says "Action" for you to begin.

And added to all of that is a pain in the ass who shows up with a black slate in his hands, who plants himself in front of the camera and then retreats, also yelling.

And so, numerous times, I started when I shouldn't have. That bothered them. But they're the ones making things complicated. Why not just say "Let's go" and leave it at that?

On top of it, Horse Mouth kept bossing us around: do this, do that, like this, not like that. The thing that did my head in the most was how many times she yelled "Cut." Sometimes, you haven't even said bismillah* in your head when you hear Horse Mouth with her megaphone yelling for you to stop.

It doesn't bother her, she doesn't care. All day, she hides out behind her black box that looks like the Kaaba* and she does the director thing, staring at her screen. All you can see is her legs sticking out of the bottom. And since her ears are covered with enormous headphones, she talks loudly. If you've been smoking hash or drinking, you might confuse her with God, giving orders, always unseen.

And there's a chick with her, a real brat!

The script girl, they call her. They hired her just to piss us off. That's her entire job. She carries a notebook, she wears glasses, and she watches you. If you make a tiny little mistake or say something that's not exactly like in the script, she comes and scolds you, like a schoolteacher. You should have seen what she did to the guy who was in charge of the decor ...

But I think he deserved it. He's a real cheapskate! He made them a shitty set: you've never seen anything so ordinary. The scene takes place in a bedroom. And that lazy asshole did the bare minimum. He set up a bed, a tiny shit-colored rug, and a table with an ashtray full of butts and beers. That's it. And while we, the actors, took a break between two scenes, he, to justify his salary, would approach the bed and start to smooth the creases. Or he would pick up and move the ashtray. Is that what he calls work?

Anyway, other than him, it's clear that these people are professionals. Everyone knows what they have to do. No one wastes time. The camera guy, you should see how his camera suits him. And the one who holds the sound broom, he's enormous. And there's one guy, a foreigner, also blond. Incredible. Of all of them, he's the one who really impresses me. He's very small, skinny, he looks like a baby goat. And with his minuscule arms, he moves those huge lights! They're each twice his weight. He holds them by a large, heavy rod. I was so intrigued by him that I screwed up a scene.

While I was telling Kaïs Brahim to go fuck himself, I noticed that guy moving something and it distracted me. You could only see the bottom of his feet beneath a gigantic light. I found it incredible that someone so frail could carry something so big, so instead of insulting Kaïs Brahim as I was supposed to, I said to him, my eyes on the baby goat, "Repeat what you just said?" That's a sentence that comes later in the script. Of course, that bitch Horse Mouth didn't let it slide. And she said that we would take a break. Fine by me because then I was able to follow Maaizou.* That's what I call the baby goat. I wanted to see the rod up close to know if it was plastic or iron. He handed me the rod. It was really iron.

Even though it was a bit of a mess today, these people know what they're doing. I hadn't understood this morning what the giant guy was director of, and I thought that maybe he was even Horse

Mouth's boss, but that's not it at all. In fact, here, they say director like we say maallem.* It means that you're a professional of your trade. That you're the most gifted and you know the most things. And given how skilled these people are, they're almost all maallem of something.

If you had been with me today your mouth would have been hanging open in astonishment. It was really something, after all.

SATURDAY THE 30TH

Ten more days of filming and then it's over. It's four in the morning and I can't get up. Never in my life have I had to wake up so early.

Samira is lucky. She could saw through the entire Maâmora* Forest she snores so much. Her arm— which hangs over the bed—is perpetually at risk of knocking over the coffee machine they brought me when they saw that I was fundamentally incompatible with their schedule. You should see the bedroom now! It's as if I've always lived here.

The fridge is about to burst. Inside there are Dannon yogurts, bread, Siviana,* mortadella, Laughing Cow, and pineapple juice. And desserts of all kinds and all colors. During filming, I always tell them to set some aside so that I can take them home with me in the afternoon.

Today is not like the other days. We're going to film in a special location. Next to the market. My market. In the street that leads to Alpha 55.*

"Jmiaa? Knock knock! Jmiaa?"

"*Oui?*" I answer, walking toward the door and speaking softly so as not to wake up Samira.

Now, they don't say anything to me when she stays with me, but after our first night together here, they did everything in their power to get rid of her. I understand why, because when Samira showed up, she brought trouble with her.

The first day, the assholes from the hotel wouldn't let her go up. She entered the lobby and instead of continuing on her way, that idiot stood there with her mouth open, gawking at the decor. She was especially amazed by the horse, she said. While she was swallowing flies, one of the mountains that guards the entryway approached her and asked her where she was going.

That's how it always is. No matter where you go. If the guard dogs at the door don't know you or if you don't bribe them, they give you trouble. That's how it is at the nightclub, at the police station, at the schools, everywhere.

Samira told him that she had a meeting with someone. The guy told her that only the guests were permitted to enter. Samira insisted. He repeated what he had already said. And then I don't know exactly what

Samira answered. But it didn't go over so well with the guy, who grabbed her by the arm. Right when she was about to cause a scene and start yelling, Horse Mouth arrived. He got lucky, that guy. If Samira had let loose on him, I don't care how big he is, he would still be hiding out in a hole somewhere. Samira was very pleased by the room; we settled in, we had a few glasses of wine, and she left.

The next day, she came back. We had another few glasses, and then, since we were feeling good, we decided to go out. Shooting didn't start until 11 the next day. We got in a taxi and left for the coast. We said that we'd have some fun, have a few glasses, and head back.

The only thing I went back to was that asshole Bouchaïb. We had only just arrived in one of those clubs on the coast when I saw him. He was at a table covered in bottles. Saïd and Belaïd, the inseparable balls that follow him like a shadow, were sitting and laughing and around them was a gaggle of girls, subpar whores. I elbowed Samira's stomach, nodding at the table with my chin. I wanted to leave but she dragged me inside. Before I could react, I found myself at the bar.

We sat down. A pole hid us from their view. I decided that as soon as I had an opportunity to leave, I would.

Then, Belaïd saw us. He got up to go to the bathroom. After that, it was inevitable. Less than five minutes after he had returned to his spot, that bear Bouchaïb and his fat stomach came over. He had blown up even more, and with his new mustache he looked like a police chief. He insisted that we go sit with them. That shithead Samira wanted to party and drink for free. And I followed her, like an idiot.

When we arrived at his table, he shooed away the girls who were sitting with them like you would dust off a rug. With their death glares, they spit in our faces. Bouchaïb acted like everything was normal between us. He sat me next to him and shifted his arm behind my back, placing his hand on the top of my thigh. We drank more than we should have. The problem was that with filming, I hadn't been drinking much. And so again, the inevitable happened.

Bouchaïb let his hand rummage around in places I didn't want it to go. I felt an electric shock run through me. As soon as he started to knead under my djellaba, I went into a fit of rage. I couldn't stand for him to touch me there, as if it were his. And at that moment, chaos broke loose.

It went from an ordinary, chill scene to a racket like you've never seen before. Glass broke, tables were overturned. Samira lost it, Belaïd took off. Bouchaïb bit his lip and his fist crashed down onto my face. My nails dug into his cheek. Hands pulling. Hair. Screams, noise, spitting, blood. And then all of it mixed together. They threw all of us out onto the sidewalk. After that, the night passed quickly. From the sidewalk to the van, from the van to the police station, from the police station to the cell. From the cell to Samira's, and then the muezzin calling the dawn prayer. And through it all, no trace of Chaïba. Chaïba had gone on his way. Chaïba had kept going without looking back at the muck he'd left in his wake. Chaïba had given me a peace offering by inviting me to his table. Chaïba gets what he wants. Where he wants it. Chaïba had lent me money when I was sick. All that meat, those thighs, that bounty overflowing from my chest, it all belongs to him.

But when things went south, Chaïba took off. He bribed the uniforms and returned to Hajar or to who knows what slob to dump his load. He bribed them and calmly stumbled to his car. He gave them enough so that they wouldn't keep us too late into the night but not enough for them to leave us alone entirely. Fucking asshole!

If he sees my face again, I swear to you, my name isn't Jmiaa.

After the fog of dawn, the first thing I remember is Horse Mouth and her teeth bent over me in Samira's room. Fuck, that was another incredible mess. It was four in the afternoon or something. It was way past the time I was supposed to be on set. Now it was time to shut up. To listen and nod yes. She was so dramatic. She didn't scream or anything. No. She was speaking softly but her entire body was tense, as if another person was about to come out of her. And a vein that had always remained calmly in the middle of her forehead had popped out. When she was done, she told me that we would see each other back at the hotel, and she showed herself out. I said nothing. I wasn't there. My head was spinning, heavy. It had been a long time since I'd been in such a state. It had been a long time since I'd found my-self face-to-face with the black screen of the televi-sion. And the reflection of Hamid counting his bills while my stomach jumped into my chest.

I was afraid. And I didn't answer Horse Mouth. All I could do was prop myself on my elbows and glance at my face in the mirror. By a stroke of luck, the only visible trace was the kohl that had run down to my mouth. You should have seen the fuss I made to Samira when she woke up. I had been going about my business and she had dragged me into that shitty mess. I had just started on set. And I had sworn that I would no longer do anything with that asshole. Fortunately we had left all our energy in the cell, otherwise I swear she and I would have ended up swinging at each other.

In the end, like everything else, it passed. Samira and I calmed down. And Horse Mouth let it go. But it was difficult to make up for that shitty night.

The next day, when I returned to the set, no one could stand me. These people, when they can't stand you, they don't sulk or insult you or any of the things that normal people do. They just look at you sideways and don't speak to you, that's all.

That day, they all twisted their necks looking in the other direction when I passed. Horse Mouth said that because of me, all of filming had stopped, and they had lost money. They're so full of themselves, you can't even imagine.

I'm going to tell you something—because I've lived it now: all that structure turns you into an asshole.

"Knock knock. Jmiaa? Are you awake?" says the voice, in Arabic this time, from behind the door.

Even though I can't see him, I know he has his mouth pressed up against the wood as if it were glued to my tits. It's Maaizou, the baby goat. He's become infatuated with me, the poor guy. Every morning, he comes to wake me up. I think he's afraid I won't show up or that I'll have disappeared into the night again. Or maybe someone asked him to do it, I don't know. He's started to learn Arabic. He knows how to say all the words he needs to say: "Are you awake?" "Are you hungry?" "Do you need anything?" And he speaks it well, for a foreigner.

Today is his lucky day. Even though I have to be up before dawn and even though I'm struggling, I am indeed up.

"It's fine, you can go, I'm awake."

Next to me, he's like a kid. I surpass him in height, in breadth, in width, in everything. His head is barely bigger than one of my breasts. He doesn't care. As soon as he has a free moment, he flocks to me.

He wants me to teach him Arabic, he said. My ass that's what he wants! But that's not my problem. I don't do anything with him. They told me I couldn't work during filming. So I'm not working.

Fine by me. Maaizou spoils me and I give him nothing in return. Nothing, not even a blow job. And Samira benefits from it too. Every day, he brings us something. I have so many perfumes I'm sick of them. I think he might be a bit of a dope.

"It's fine. We'll see each other on set," I say to him.

I speak to him slowly. And I add gestures so that he'll understand. He leaves, saying goodbye in Arabic. Despite everything, he's actually pretty sharp. He's a quick learner.

*Y*ou should see the faces of the people around me. Their mouths are all hanging open. All of them. And since it's Saturday, everyone is here. It must be two in the afternoon. The day's been hot. And long. We've been shooting since six in the morning and we still have about two hours left to go.

I'm standing next to a store they've made to look like a jewelry store. It's the store that belongs to that bitch who normally sells clothing. Next to the bakery. Kaïs Brahim and I are waiting for the crew to tell us to start. I'm having a hard time concentrating.

I've started to get used to the circus and all the lines I can't remember. But today, it's too much for me.

First off, they've blocked the street. No one can come in, no one can leave. They put up barriers to stop the cars so that we can film without interruption. I'm not used to seeing the street like this. Normally, it's like a souk, and now, even though they've retained some of the chaos, I'm thrown off by the order they've imposed. And the cops, there are too many of them. Everywhere you look, there they are. Two days ago, some crazy guy blew himself up in a café in Marrakech. The guy got up one morning, put a bomb in his bag, walked into a café and boom! That's what his deranged brain told him to do. Who knows why. It was in that super famous square, Jemaa el-Fnaa. I've never been before but they show it on TV all the time. There are snake charmers, fortune-tellers, orange-juice sellers, snails, all sorts of things. An insane amount of tourists have gone there. Since that day, the Dutch haven't shut up about it. Maaizou said they're afraid of being blown up too.

And so, at noon, they completely surrounded the restaurant they rented out for lunch. No one went in, no one went out without being searched. But nothing happened. Even though I'm starting to get used to it, I still don't like for there to be so many cops around.

Today—serves them right—they're going to suffer. Because my supporters make the apaches of Raja* look like babies. All the people I know and even some I don't know are here.

They're all behind the barrier. There's Bachir the grocer, Fouzia, Rabia, Mina the elderly woman, that whore Hajar and her girlfriend, Najia the hairdresser. There's Okraïcha the second-floor neighbor, who stopped to see what was going on. There's the blind bat Robio, who is selling socks today. They were all wondering where I'd disappeared to, and now, here I am, before their eyes, starring in a film. Even Hamid came to see.

We reconciled this morning. When I arrived at dawn, he had just finished his night shift at the garage. He waved to me from afar. I had just stepped out of wardrobe. I let him come in to say hello. He asked me to forgive him for not having come to see me after the accident. He said that our friendship went too far back for anything to tarnish it. I told him it was okay, that there was no problem, that God knew how to forgive everything. Between us, you know what? I gave in. Because I can't afford to waste time being angry with idiots like him now.

Houcine is also here, next to the market. Hiding under his baseball cap. He must be dying to know what on earth I'm doing here. First the accident, then my disappearance since I moved to the hotel, and now this. I'll call him when I'm done filming to explain it to him. But honestly, he can go fuck himself. All that matters is that I get him his money, right?

There are so many people that I can't even see them all. They're squeezed against the barriers, like on the news when the king passes. And the mo-qaddem* is sitting over there, on the set with us. I had never seen his teeth before today. Normally he greets you with a grimace distorting his unfortunate face. When he saw me and realized that I was in the film, you should have seen his expression. As if he were at the door of paradise and I held the keys. When he approached me, I greeted him. I sat him at a table, one of the ones they put on the sidewalk to the right of the set so that the actors and technicians can rest. I told the assistant to bring him a coffee and I gave him a cigarette. When I took out the pack of Marlboros, his jaw dropped. What, did he think I was going to pump my lungs full of those disgusting Marvels all my life?

Samira is sitting at the table next to him. I asked that she join the actors and the team today. Horse Mouth didn't protest. Samira's wearing a djellaba that I've never seen her in before. I don't know where she pulled that one out from, the minx. It's yellow. Like the inside of an egg. The color of her hair actually. And with a slit in the front! She's holding a Fanta in one hand and in the other she's taking a drag, flaunting in front of all those watching. It's an incredible spectacle. The moqaddem doesn't know whether to stare at Samira's thighs or at what's going on around him.

"Let's go!"

Jaafar tells us to take our places. We're going to film the scene where we enter the jewelry store to scout out the location and plan our heist. Kaïs is a knockout, and they've dressed me in a fantastic outfit! So that the jeweler wouldn't recognize me, they changed my clothes, my hairdo, my makeup, everything. They put me in a short brown wig, a bob. And my ensemble is somewhere between green and brown, with pants and a matching vest. They put me in a white blouse and I'm carrying a handbag.

I'm pretending to be a teacher. And Kaïs is my fiancé, and we're entering the store to choose a ring for me. The people watching us can't believe it's me. I really blow them away.

"Action!"

Horse Mouth has spoken. Now it's my turn.

"You go in first and I'll follow you?" I say to Kaïs before we reach the jeweler's door.

"Listen, we already talked about this. I'll go first and I'll open the door for you to go in," answers Kaïs, passing me to reach the jeweler's.

"..."

I have to say something. I don't know what. I forget. Kaïs turns toward me. He stares at me. He's waiting for me to say my line. Behind him, Fouzia's head and neck are bent backward, she's laughing so hard at seeing me like this. I can't remember my line. Fuck, I can't remember my line.

"Cut!"

Horse Mouth orders the cameraman to stop.

"Let's start over."

And she turns toward me:

"Jmiaa, focus, please."

I remember. I have to say: "But that wasn't a good plan." I get back in my starting position. "Action!"

"You go in first and I'll follow you?"

"Listen, we already talked about this. I'll go first and I'll open the door for you to go in."

That bitch Fouzia is still laughing. She's still in the same spot as before. Even Bachir is laughing now.

"No, not like that. Let's go this way," I respond, turning to Kaïs.

Kaïs looks at me without saying anything. I don't remember exactly what I just said but I don't think it was right.

"Cut!"

Horse Mouth again. I look at her. She pokes her head out of her black box. Her look signals to me that I need to focus and her mouth says calmly, "Take your places again. From the top."

Kaïs turns his back to me to return to his place. It's hot in this outfit. And this vest is restricting me.

Especially around my waist. Sheesh, it's really tight. And this wig is starting to get on my nerves. It's making me hot. And I know myself. When I have things clinging to me all over, it gets on my nerves. But with all these people watching me, I can't complain.

"Action!" says Horse Mouth.

We start filming.

"You go in first and I'll follow you?" I say.

"Listen, we already talked about this. I'll go first and I'll open the door for you to go in."

"Action!"

What is this shit?

"Action! Action! Hello? Yes, Madame Rhimou?"

I don't know where that fucking noise is coming from. When I look behind the barrier, I see some people laughing, others looking around like me, turning their heads to see where the sound is coming from.

"Action!"

It's coming from my left. Behind Bachir, that idiot Mbarka, the old woman, screaming like she does when the bin-ou-bin pass and she shows them her ass. She walks, swaying, toward the center of the crowd. Her arms are on her hips and she yells as she walks.

"Action!"

No one knows what to look at anymore. Should they look at me, where the real film is going on, or at the other film that the crazy lady is directing over there? She walks like a goose. She's hiked up her djellaba above her knees, holding it at her waist. And the lipstick she's slathered on is all over her mouth.

The others laugh, looking from her to Horse Mouth to see how she's going to react. They understand that she's the boss, who says what to do and what not to do. Horse Mouth is at a loss.

She's crazy, that Mbarka. I look at Samira and I barely have time to laugh before a cop grabs the old woman by the collar and drags her away. She falls backward, directly onto her ass. Another cop arrives to help his friend.

Mbarka doesn't understand what's going on, and with all that lipstick, all we can see of her face is her mouth in the shape of a big "O." Samira and I are on the ground we're laughing so hard. The entire neighborhood is on the ground. The cops take her to the end of the street to smack her around a little while she kicks frantically in the air.

"Hey, no, no, what are you doing? Leave her alone!"

Horse Mouth has jumped out of her seat, she's running toward the cop. Fuck, what is her problem?

"Leave her alone! No! No!"

Horse Mouth gets to the barrier quick as lightning. She tries to climb over it. Fouzia steps back and watches to see whether she'll manage to get to the other side or not. One of the cops stands behind Horse Mouth.

"No, madame, leave it, we'll take care of it," he says to her in French.

She continues to jump like a madwoman trying to cross the barrier. The cop doesn't know what to do anymore.

"No, leave it, madame, leave it."

He speaks to her politely, the son of a bitch. This guy who normally pulls out his club as soon as he sees people throwing themselves over barriers doesn't dare grab her by the arm, the moron. His hand keeps extending toward Horse Mouth's elbow, but he doesn't touch her.

"Return to your place, madame, we'll take care of her," he says, looking at her with adoring eyes.

"Is that so? What do you mean, you'll take care of her? Look how they're treating her!"

Horse Mouth points her finger toward the crazy lady, who is still being dragged backward by the two cops, punching at the air and screaming at them to let her go.

A guy named Khalid who works with us on the set gets involved. Khalid grabs Horse Mouth by the elbow. I sit down next to Samira, I have a sip of her Fanta and light a cigarette. We're not filming, might as well kick back and watch the show. The moqaddem has gotten up. Now, everyone surrounds Horse Mouth.

The Dutch have joined her league for the defense of human rights. The Moroccans and the cops try to explain to them that we have to get back to filming. That nothing's going to happen to the old woman. Even Fouzia and Rabia get involved.

"No, madame, you have to go over there," says Fouzia very seriously to Horse Mouth in French.

All the girls burst out laughing. Samira and I do too. It encourages her.

"Yes, madame, you have to go over there. They're waiting for you," she adds, still in French.

Khalid tells Horse Mouth and her team to stand aside, he says that he's going to take care of it. And he goes to talk to the cops. He turns back toward Horse Mouth to tell her that everything's okay. She tells him that they're not going to resume filming until the elderly woman—that's how she describes the crazy lady—has come back from where the cops dragged her.

Khalid wants to smack her, it's obvious.

Honestly, in his place, I'd want to do the same thing. She's really a pain in the ass sometimes, that Horse Mouth. But Khalid says nothing and goes to take care of the problem. There must have been blue bills* involved because immediately after, the police let go of the crazy woman.

Mbarka walks back toward us, adjusting her djellaba and turning around to make sure the cops aren't following her. She understands that it's because of the film people that they let her go so she shoots the cops a snooty look. Horse Mouth approaches her, I don't know what she says to her but Khalid opens the barriers to the madwoman to let her in. What bullshit!

They've even given her a chair now. And they brought her a Fanta too. Bullshit! And look at her! Now she's playing the victim in front of them. She's showing the scars on her legs to Horse Mouth. And the scars on her elbows. And the cold sore underneath her lipstick which she wipes off on the sleeve of her djellaba. She's out of her mind! And all you people who fuss over her and her antics are out of your minds too! It's your pockets you should be fussing over. She'll clean you out before you can even say "aye."

But I'm going to let it go because it's not my problem. And let that crazy woman live it up while she still can. Because those cops over there, trust me, they'll be nice and calm until the Dutch pack up their circus, and then they'll make her spit back up that Fanta she just drank.

"Jmiaa, get in position, we're going to start again."

It's Jaafar. About time! I fix my pants and my blouse and I let out a big sigh to show everyone that they're giving me a headache with all their crap. Children! Every last one of them.

May

THURSDAY THE 5TH

Yesterday, for the first time since we started filming, I spent my day off in the neighborhood. You should have seen how they welcomed me.

First I went to the house to check out my room and make sure everything was in its place. I stayed for fifteen minutes and then went back down. I had put on a new djellaba. Green, with yellow trim. And I was wearing new sandals too, and I had my hair down.

What I'm trying to say is, I looked good. And I didn't even have time to get down the stairs before I was accosted by people who wanted to speak to me. The first person I saw was Okraïcha. Guess what: she invited me to have tea at her place. It was the first time I'd been in her home. As soon as we were seated, Samira and I, she served us msemens, honey, olive oil, olives, and she made a perfectly sweet tea.

Her daughter was there, and even her mother, who is living with her right now while she takes care of some things at the courthouse.

I showed her that she's not the only one from a good family. Samira was on her best behavior too. When I wanted to leave because it was getting late and there were other people I wanted to see, I nodded at her and she announced our departure. Samira thanked Okraïcha for welcoming us and told her we had to leave because we still had a lot of things to do. That I had people to see and that they were waiting for me back at the hotel to prepare for tomorrow's shoot. I acquiesced, adding another layer of excuses. Okraïcha said that she understood and that we were always welcome, that it was a big day for her to have entertained us. She and her daughter accompanied us to the hallway. She's kind, that woman, it turns out. We just didn't know her before.

Then we went into the street, where it was total madness. Everyone came to greet me, everyone wanted to have tea with me. Everyone wanted to know what it was like on the other side.

I had expected that they would assail me. I had brought a two-hundred-dirham bill to pay for a round. We went to a café with the girls. I brought them to Abdelali's place. There were six of us. Samira and I, Rabia, Fouzia, and two others you don't know. Najiba and Kebira. We sat inside, we ordered two big teapots and every kind of pastry they had. We laughed, we drank, we ate.

I told them about the film crew. All the necessary preparation. The script, the makeup, the lights, the outfits, the memorization. I taught them things they would never have learned otherwise. And I also told them what people say about me over there. Like the day when Maaizou told me he had never seen anyone assimilate as quickly as I had.

Their mouths were agape the whole time I was speaking. Abdelali and his server too. They pretended to be setting the tables next to us so they could listen to our conversation. I took pity on them and raised my voice so that they could hear without straining too much.

On my phone, I showed the girls my photos from the hotel, by the horse, at the pool, the restaurant table. With the Dutch people. With Horse Mouth. With Hasna and Wafaa doing my makeup and hair. With the costume designer, the giant blonde. With Nasser, the driver, next to the car. I showed them all the photos I'd taken. Of my hotel room too. Everywhere.

We must have stayed at the café for a full two hours. When we wanted to pay, Abdelali refused to bring me the bill. I insisted. But he refused to take a single rial. Before leaving, I told him that I would tell the film crew—who I'm friendly with now—to come to his café for their meals. And we left.

I continued to make my way through the neighborhood, talking to the girls. We went to the market, the bakery, the avenue, Pommercy. I gave everyone a bit of my time. Even Hamid.

But when I walked by Hajar, who was sitting on the steps—like a turd drying in the sun—I looked straight through her and her friend. Let her go run and tell Bouchaïb what I've become so that he'll regret ever leaving with her and daring to raise a hand to me. You know, I can forgive everyone, except for him. I can forgive Hamid, my husband who took off and left me. Mouy, who kept my daughter and turned her back on me as if she hadn't brought me into the world. Houcine, who for all these years has taken money that I earned through my own hard work. I'll forgive all of them. But I'll never forgive him.

FRIDAY THE 20TH

Today, it's Friday. I'm in my room, in town. We finished filming.

They gave me three and a half million, all the costumes they had made for me, the makeup, the bags and scarves. They took good care of me.

Before we left, there was a big party at the hotel. And we spent our last night together. It was barely a week ago, but it seems like so long ago, like it never happened.

At the end of the night, we took a group photo.

Horse Mouth brought me a framed print of it yesterday. In a black frame, simple and thin, but the photo is magnificent, and I hung it on the wall opposite my mattress.

Everyone is in it. We're all standing behind the pool, on the roof. You can see the water shining, the lights, the candles...everything.

I'm standing in the middle, next to Horse Mouth. I'm wearing a long, red dress that I bought the other day in Maârif. Kaïs is on the other side of Horse Mouth. And everyone else is around us. We're all laughing. I had just let out a spectacular youyou. You can still see it on my face.

Today, Horse Mouth took the plane. The Dutch left, the Moroccans scattered. Everyone is gone.

There's just me, lingering here.

And I have no clue what to make of it all.

2013

April

TUESDAY THE 23RD

You'll never be able to guess where I am. Never. I'm on a plane.

On a plane that's bringing me to America. Yes, America. The United States of America, as they say.

And this is the second plane I've taken today. The first brought me from the Mohammed V airport to France, where I changed planes. And now I'm on this one.

I'm sitting next to the window. It's tiny, round. Outside, it's pouring. When we took off from Casablanca, the sun was beating down hard. God only knows what the weather will be like in America.

Saïda, the niece of Fatema, our neighbor in Berrechid, who lives over there, told me it's cold. Sometimes, it snows so much that the schools close for an entire week. So I brought a big wool shawl, thick socks, and Mouy's green winter djellaba, the one that she had made last year before going to see her sister in the village.

Speaking of Mouy, you should have seen her just now at the airport, the poor thing. She cried her heart out when we said goodbye. Neither my daughter, nor my brothers, nor their wives, nor their children, not even the policeman who was standing there, managed to calm her down.

She didn't stop until I reached the customs area, where they only allow in the people with passports and tickets. She stood there, sheepish, gaze distant and hollow. Put yourself in her place: your only daughter is going to America; God knows what she'll find over there... I understand. I asked forgiveness from everyone before leaving. You never know, something might happen on the way and then I'd have to answer for it up above.

At the airport, the woman who was next to me as I went through security felt sorry for me when she saw my mother in such a state. The poor lady, she's a good woman. She lives in France with her husband and her children. She's been there for thirty years. Now her children are grown up and she came to Morocco because her mother, God bless her soul, is sick.

I met her where you drop off your suitcases for them to be loaded onto the plane. Since I wasn't sure how it worked, I asked her and she told me to follow her. She showed me everything. And when we arrived in France, she brought me to the hallway that led me to where I boarded the plane I'm on now. I swear to you that without her, never in my life would I have gotten here. Also, she gave me her number and told me to go see her one day if I'm ever in France.

God only knows what it will be like in America! I'm going to a town called San Francisco. Horse Mouth showed it to me on a world map. It's on the other side of the planet. You cross the entire Atlantic Ocean and when you reach the American coast, you still have the same amount of distance to go to get to San Francisco as what you've already traveled. And only then do you arrive. But I'm still a long way from there.

We've just finished eating. I really went to town on the tray they served us for dinner. I inhaled everything. To tell the truth, I'm living this to the fullest. Anyone else would do the same. Especially when you know the price of the ticket. I didn't pay out of my own pocket but a woman who works for a travel agency in town told me how much it was. A million eight hundred rials, can you believe it? Now, I'm going to watch the film that Horse Mouth and I picked out before I take a nap. I chose a Hindu film that looks incredible. Shah Rukh Khan* is in it. And that other bombshell whose name I can't remember.

I have a television screen to myself, on the back of the chair of the person in front of me. I took off my shoes, I put on the socks they gave me and I reclined my chair back as far as it goes. I even covered myself up with the blanket they give you in the beginning, when you board.

You know, now I'm settled in and starting to get used to all of it, but this morning at the airport, I didn't know what I was doing. Even though Samira and I had tried to prepare for the trip. And even though we said that I would be careful, there are moments when it's all so unbelievable that my mouth takes me by surprise and my tongue starts flapping all on its own.

Who would have thought that I, Jmiaa, would be going to America because a film I acted in was accepted as part of a festival? When Horse Mouth contacted me from the Netherlands three months ago to tell me that the film would screen in America, I didn't believe her. And even now that I'm on the plane, I still don't believe it. Even now.

I remember what I was doing at the exact moment when she called. It was a Friday. Since the end of filming, I had resumed work, my two-bit life and the patterns that go along with it. I spent the money from the film. The cameras were a thing of the past. Abdelali's generosity had dried up. Okraïcha's kindness was no more. The moqaddem's smiles had disappeared. There was nothing left. There was only me, my costumes, and the framed, lonely photo on my bedroom wall.

If I was anything like Halima, you would have found me crying about my fate, staring at the photo, a river of snot coming out of my nose... But anyway, to each her own.

That Friday, I was drinking a beer and it was seven o'clock on the dot.

"Hello?"

"Hey, Jmiaa, today is a big day. Pack your things!"

Horse Mouth was yelling into the telephone. By the time she explained to me what was going on and I finally understood, she had already hung up. I was in shock.

It wasn't until the next day that I started to realize. First I called back Horse Mouth to make sure I hadn't imagined any of it. With all the pills in my system, you never know. And after that call, when it had finally sunk in, I made moves, and everything moved with me.

I withdrew all the money I had and bribed everyone I had to for a passport. And before that, I had to get a new national ID card. I scattered my money around to stack the odds in my favor. The caid,* the moqaddem, the guy at the wilaya,* the friends of Samira's guy Aziz, everyone. Nearly everything

I had disappeared in the process. I called people I knew and people I didn't know. People I've fucked and people who've fucked me.

I couldn't tell you who did what, but I can tell you that it worked.

And in the end, all those days I spent moving heaven and earth passed without me realizing it. I didn't start to really grow afraid until I received my passport. I was afraid that, for one reason or another, it would all come crashing to a halt. The day when I went to the US consulate for my visa appointment—and before I got to the guy who asks you questions—I must have lost ten pounds of sweat alone.

Every time someone spoke to me, I would tell myself: "All right, now they're going to stop me." And every time I passed to the next stage, I would say to myself, "I made it this time, but I'll be stopped next time." That's how it went until I was sitting in front of that man with the red mustache, the American who asks you questions about why you want the visa and what you're going to do over there. He speaks to you in Moroccan. Not in English. They speak to you in Moroccan at the US consulate. Isn't that incredible?

I lined up in the street, where there are police and those big metal machines that look like dumpsters filled with flowers. You know, the ones they installed the day after another crazy guy blew himself up in front of the consulate a while back. I lined up a second time on the other side of the street, behind the barrier, where there's another swarm of cops who check your papers and your appointment. I passed.

I lined up behind a desk at the entrance, where there's a donkey who speaks to you as if he were the white Obama. I passed.

Next, I followed the flood of people until I got to the place where they search you and take your phone. I passed there too.

I don't know how I did it, but I passed every time. And when I reached the guy with the red mustache, I was afraid like never before in my life.

When he was finished with his questions, he told me that they would return my passport along with my visa in two days and he smiled at me. I stayed there waiting for the next thing. I didn't budge until he said again, smiling even wider, that I was free to go. And then, afraid he would change his mind, I grabbed my things and took off.

I think it was the sura that I repeated in my head before reaching his desk that blinded him. Or else the purse filled with nigella seed that the faqih gave me made an invisible wall between me and the others so they didn't see me. Or else maybe I did a good deed one day and I just don't remember. I have no clue.

In any event, the guy hardly asked me any questions. He looked at the papers that Horse Mouth gave me, he saw my airplane ticket, he asked if I was leaving my daughter at my mother's, and he told me to have a good trip. That was it.

After that, two more days passed, I picked up my passport and I went to the bus station. I bought a ticket and I went to Mouy's. Directly. Without stopping along the way. It had been two years since I'd last seen or spoken to her. Two years.

As for Samia, I swear if I hadn't carried her in my stomach, I would never have recognized her. When I saw her again, it was like someone hit me. All at once, I felt the weight of those two years. Day to day, you don't have the time to reflect, but there are moments when, for whatever reason, you feel things. And in that moment, I felt that I had missed Samia.

In Berrechid, everything was exactly as I'd left it. Including the key for the front door on the sill.

I arrived at a time when I knew that Mouy would be alone. I showed up in the living room like an apparition. Before she'd had a chance to raise her head to see who'd entered, I was already kissing her feet with the passport raised in my right hand.

Without stopping to catch my breath, I asked for her blessing. I wouldn't go anywhere, I wouldn't take any plane without her blessing. Not for America, or Sweden, or anywhere else. I wouldn't go to the film festival in America even though I'm the star of the film. I wouldn't go to America to find a job. I wouldn't go to America to build a future for myself and for my daughter. I wouldn't go to make enough money to send home substantial payments each month. I wouldn't go to begin another life. I would kiss her feet and stay there until she gave me her blessing. And only then would I leave.

As I spoke, I handed her an envelope full of money for her to keep in case something happened to me during the trip.

I cried that day. I cried as long as I needed to and when I was done, she lifted me up and she forgave me. That's how I left.

WEDNESDAY THE 24TH

Holy shit, we're in America. We've arrived. We're driving on a freeway like you've never seen before. I can't count the number of lanes there are on each side of the barrier that separates the two directions. Four? Five? Six? My neck can't keep up. Cars are rushing from all directions. You're asking yourself where that car came from and then suddenly another one overtakes you, leaving you in the dust. It's as if there were a giant behind us, thighs open, giving birth to one after another, her spawn in a hurry to join the world. Fatema's niece is full of shit. Cold, in America? There's a sun bright enough to blind you and every other motherfucker on the planet! Horse Mouth has on her black sunglasses and is looking through the window, with that perpetual smile on her lips. That idiot forgot the bag with all the cartons of cigarettes we bought on the plane, but she doesn't seem to care, the dummy. Her lips are happy.

Mine too, I think. Barely out of the airport, I smoked two of my own cigarettes, one after another. They grounded me.

Holy shit, I'm in America. I can't believe it. I have arrived in America.

And in front of us, look at that bridge! No, it's not a bridge. It's bridges. Going in every direction. Like the legs of a spider. We pass under one.

To the left and to the right, the gray walls begin again. Since leaving the airport, sometimes we catch glimpses of the city, its trees, houses, stores like Marjane. But sometimes we see nothing but walls.

God only knows what's behind them. What's certain is that it's not like our country. It's not possible that they'd have things to hide here. It's not possible that they would have corrugated iron, filth, and rags to conceal.

"What's behind those walls?" I ask Horse Mouth.

"What walls?" she asks, turning her head toward me. "Those?" and she points to the wall with her finger.

I nod my head yes. Frowning slightly to signify that it's nothing, she says, "It's nothing. It's just residential neighborhoods. They put up walls so the residents have privacy."

Straight from the Horse's Mouth

Bullshit. No one lives behind those walls. Since we got in the car earlier, I haven't seen any bridges for people to cross or any other openings for people to leave through.

If I knew how to speak English, I would have asked the taxi driver. He would know what's behind them. Taxi drivers always know. Because she lives in the Netherlands, she thinks she knows everything. Hey, Horse Mouth, wake up, this is America! There are things that even you don't understand.

Fuck, my head is spinning. I don't know what time it is. I asked that crazy woman when we arrived. She said it was Tuesday, 6:30 in the evening. But we left Tuesday morning at 10:30 am and the hands of the clock have already made their way around the dial since then. I don't know how she came up with that math. I've been trying to add it up, I can't figure it out.

"Look over here. It's beautiful, isn't it?" says Horse Mouth.

I lean over to see the buildings with the sea in the background to our right. And on the other side, in the distance, there's a mountain like the one in Agadir. The one with the inscription "God, Country, King."

I've been to Agadir once in my life. I was so drunk that I don't remember anything except for that mountain. In any case, it's the only thing anyone remembers when they go there.

On this mountain, there's writing like in our country. In white, directly on the earth.

"What's the motto in this country?" I ask Horse Mouth, showing her the writing on the mountain.

She turns her head to see.

"Huh? Oh, that!" and she laughs. "It's not their motto. It says, 'South San Francisco The Industrial City.'"

"Hmmm." I turn back to my window.

Idiot!

May

Wow wow wow, the food they have here. You should see the portions they give you. I didn't hesitate for a second when Horse Mouth asked me what I wanted to eat this morning: a traditional breakfast, that's what I wanted. Something to fill my stomach, one hundred percent American. They really know how to eat here.

If you ever come here one day, that's what you have to order. I have eggs. An omelette filled with vegetables. I wouldn't even be able to describe everything that's in it because there's so much. Zucchini, herbs, green red and yellow peppers, onions. There's even tomato. And on the side, potatoes cut up into cubes, and slices of their breakfast bread. Big square slices. To be honest, I prefer our bread, but this is fine. They also bring you butter and jam for free, just because you ordered eggs. I also ordered a bowl with all kinds of fruit and Dannon yogurt.

I didn't order a pastry because I wouldn't have known where to put it, but you should have seen them. You've never seen such big pastries in your life. They're tall and have multiple layers. On the bottom, there's cream, in the middle, there's cream, on the top, there's more cream. It never ends. Sometimes they have five or even six layers.

I ordered a latte to drink. They have a crazy system here. When you order a coffee or a Coke or anything to drink—except alcohol—they refill you and refill you until you can't take it anymore. When you finish your glass, the server comes to ask if you want more. You could have twenty refills if you wanted. They do it because the people here are idiots. Even when they're in a group, they all order drinks, rather than having one and sharing it.

To be honest, I find their population a bit stupid. We might be poor but we're not stupid. They have everything they need and they don't know what to do with it. For example, if you buy something and you don't like it, or it's not the right size, or whatever other reason, you return it to the store with the packaging and your receipt and they give you back the money. Even if it's open, even if you've worn it. They don't even ask you why and they give you back all the money you paid for it.

Straight from the Horse's Mouth

Once I discovered this trick, I bought three pairs of shoes. And three bags. And I also bought two scarves and two pairs of socks. It bothers Horse Mouth because she's the one who has to talk to the cashiers to get reimbursed. I don't care. If she's been contaminated by their stupidity, how is that my problem?

In fact, I haven't spent any of the fifty dollars that Horse Mouth gives me each day. I've accumulated four thousand two hundred dirhams. Four thousand six hundred if you count today.

But that's not even the best part. Since I arrived, my favorite thing has been walking and taking photos. Downtown under the crazy tall buildings. In the Chinese neighborhood in front of a store with a giant tortoise on the door. At a restaurant, with an enormous green building behind me and a bowl of spaghetti in front of me. Next to the fountain downtown, with the statue of a woman and her two children. In the park, which goes all the way to the ocean. Next to the red bridge which they say is the most beautiful in the world. A bridge that withstands everything. Earthquakes, tsunamis, everything. There's no corner of this city in which I haven't been photographed.

There's only one thing I haven't taken a photo of. But that's for a reason. It's the homeless people. Holy shit, this city is full of homeless people. It's worse than Casa. I don't know where the hell they all come from. Since Horse Mouth always takes the photos, I made a point of telling her from the beginning: "Take photos of me wherever you want, whenever you want, but no homeless people in my photos. This is America."

"*Wbuca hnioea ilea moea coffii*?"

"Yes please," I answer, holding out my cup.

The server has come with her pitcher to ask me if I want more coffee. I told her yes, thank you. That's one of the first things I learned. That and *thank you, thank you very much, no, how much for this,* and *okay.* In French that's "merci," "merci beaucoup," "non," "combien pour cette chose," and I'm sure you understood that *okay* means "d'accord." It's like in Arabic. The people are nice here. That's why I learned all the phrases. So that I could talk to them too.

Like the other day, something too funny happened to me. I had just woken up, I wanted to smoke and we didn't have any cigarettes. Horse Mouth was dead asleep. I quickly threw on my djellaba and my sandals, grabbed my wallet and covered my head with the first scarf I could find to tame my hair. I was walking to the store behind our hotel when suddenly two guys in a red car drove past me.

They passed me and I saw the one in the passenger seat point at me and tell his friend to turn back around. When they passed in front of me again, just for a laugh, the one in front lowered the window, scowled, and said, pointing at me like he was holding a pistol: "Bam." He was a good actor, he looked serious and didn't laugh. And with his shaved head and his tattoos, he looked really mean.

But he didn't know who he was messing with. To show him that I, too, can act, I brought my hands to my heart as if I had been hit and pretended to collapse on the sidewalk.

My acting was so good both of their jaws dropped.

There's no doubt about it, if I win a prize at this festival, it's because I'm just too good.

I had my dress for the event custom-made. As soon as I knew I was coming, I went to the seamstress. It's modeled after the outfit Najat wears on the cover of her penultimate album. The one she wore again for that televised event, a long time ago. It's a pink lebssa,* with silver embroidery on the front, the collar, and the sleeves. And big gray pearls in the middle of gold flowers all along the design down the middle. With a gold sirwal,* which narrows at the ankles. And a giant belt, with no pearls because they'd fall off. It's a wild outfit.

And for it to be truly complete—and for the first time in my life—I bought matching underwear. A bra and panty ensemble. Both lace.

And like Najat, I have gold high heels and gold dangling earrings. They're not real gold, but you'd swear they were. And I'm going to do my hair exactly like hers in the photo I brought with me so I don't screw it up the day of the event.

Because, you know, we're going to be like those people at the film festival in Marrakech that they air on Al Aoula. We're going to arrive at the theater where they're hosting the festival, we're going to stop in front of everyone, we'll take photos. There will be cameras, journalists, people behind the barriers. Like on the television. We've already been to one party, the day we arrived, and it gave me an idea of what it will be like. It was in a hotel downtown. They threw a party on a roof, around a pool, like in Casa.

There were tons of people. Everyone was dressed up. Everyone was happy. There was a buffet lined up with things to eat. And a table full of booze. And everything was free.

The things I drank! Wine, beer, vodka, gin. I drank until I fell over. When we left, the black security guys had to carry me to the car.

The next day, Horse Mouth was angry at me. She said, you can't behave like that. I didn't even argue with her. I let her talk and talk. Why would they bring out all that booze if they didn't want people to party? It's not like I was a nasty drunk or got into a brawl or anything like that. I drank and I fell over, that's all.

And also, I told her, if they had given us proper food to fill us up, it wouldn't have happened. They put out bread cut in two with cold things on top. Is that a joke? But anyway, apart from that we had a great time that night. Too bad Kaïs couldn't come with us. He would have enjoyed himself. But apparently he's shooting another film at the moment.

But even without him, I had a good time. I met people, I talked, I laughed, I did it all. No, if you're thinking that I left with someone, you're wrong. Nothing like that. Here, I'm a known actress.

I tell them that at home, in Morocco, people say hello to me in the street because I'm on the television, they ask me for my autograph, everything. As if I were Najat. Who's going to tell them otherwise?

You know, after a few drinks, you start to understand what people are saying. Even if they don't speak your language. I don't know if it's because I'm sharp or if that's how it is for everyone. But what I know is that I chatted with loads of people.

There was even a guy who knew the group Horse Mouth likes, Nass El Ghiwane, remember them? Fortunately Horse Mouth made me listen to their music. Imagine the shame if I hadn't known them when an American knows them?

He had even been to Morocco. To Essaouira. He ate fish on the port. And he saw the seagulls. And he was cold because of the wind. He did a lot of things. When I saw that he knew so much about Morocco, I took off at the first opportunity. In case he exposed me.

That night, while I was speaking to people, something bizarre happened. Even though I was relaxed, I was still focused. It was my first night here and we weren't just anywhere. So a part of my brain was paying attention to what I was doing, another was working to understand what everyone was saying, and another still was observing them to see how they were behaving among themselves.

Amid all of that, I was so busy that I didn't really take the time to look around me.

Suddenly, my eyes were distracted by a light flickering in the sky. A plane, I think. I looked up. And that's when I saw. I saw everything all around us.

From where I was, I could see the entire city. All lit up. Yellows, blues, oranges, greens. Every possible color. The cars in the streets—so far below—seemed small, like toys. I couldn't even make out the people.

And behind the buildings in the distance, a bridge hovering in the air. Like an image that only exists in the mirages of your mind. Gigantic. Illuminated. A bridge like I've never seen before and like I'll never see again, I think. A bridge looming large. Imposing. Watching over the city. Proud. And for good reason.

And those buildings that soar to the sky. And the music that followed them. As if awestruck. The music wants to join them, fly away with them too.

And that sky, vast, unending, full of stars and the dreams of those now asleep.

Straight from the Horse's Mouth

And me. Me, standing under all of it. Wearing my classy teacher's costume. And my hair pinned behind my neck. With all those people around me. Put together. Well dressed and happy.

I wanted to cry. I saw all of it, I saw myself and I don't know why I wanted to cry. I don't know why.

WEDNESDAY THE 8TH

Today's the day, we're here. We're at the festival. We're sitting, waiting for the man in the suit on the stage to call the names. A woman in a long white dress is standing next to him. Sometimes it's her who speaks. It's our turn soon, Horse Mouth tells me, our turn soon.

I don't know how I managed to be sitting here on this red chair. I wanted to tell you about my entrance into the theater and the photos and the poses I did for the cameras. And my smiles and the hands I shook. But I can't. I don't even know what happened. I don't know if I smiled or not, if I posed like a peacock or not.

I'm already here, mouth agape. Sitting in front with Horse Mouth and all the others, the film people I don't know. They're talking and laughing among themselves.

I'm in a film with no sound, just buzzing all around my head and images succeeding each other. One right after another.

Everything sparkles. The women's colorful dresses. Their teeth. Their gold. Their diamonds. The white shirts worn by their men.

And my dress too, with its pink satin, its gray pearls and their reflection dancing in the light from the ceiling.

Another image. My feet keep each other company in their golden sandals, with their pearly pink nails.

And Horse Mouth to my left. In pants, black this time. And black leather boots. And a red shirt. And a silver necklace, almost as thick as her neck. And her mane, shy at being let loose tonight. She's like a frail bird.

And my neighbor, I can only see her knees. Protruding from her sequined white dress.

And her confident hands that frolic about while her mouth sets the tempo. With their red nails at the end and a diamond bracelet on her wrist. Just one bracelet. It's enough.

And in front of us, the stage. The one where the man in the suit and the woman in the white dress call you. And a podium, where those who win the prizes speak.

I can't see very well now. They've turned out the lights. The sound travels in my direction but it's still far away. They're starting to call people, I think.

My saliva struggles down my throat and my chest is too tight for my breath. I want to ask the frail bird if it's our turn but the words can't find their way out.

They snag. Headless bodies incapable of guiding their feet.

I watch her, and my eyes—which have taken pity on me—ask her: "Is it our turn?"

"Not yet," she answers.

Her hand squeezes mine. And she goes quiet.

I feel her fear. She worked hard on this film. It's her first. Her trembling lips are hanging on by her hope.

They're calling people. There are several prizes. The man who was just called for this one runs onto the stage. He's wearing a black suit, he looks magnificent, even if he's a bit pale. And even if he's not well shaved. His eyes twinkle in the light shining from above, straight onto him. The flashes of photographers. He says things. He smiles. He lifts his prize to the sky. It seems light. The man's heart seems light too.

He goes back down. They're going to call someone else.

"Is it our turn?" my eyes ask again. "Not yet," her hand replies.

The next person goes up. He doesn't know where to look. His head spins around in every direction. He says nothing. He cries. He's a man. But he's crying like a baby.

In front of the cameras. Those to the side, those in front. And even those above, affixed to the ceiling.

The cameras. The first thing I saw when I entered the theater. Standing on their tireless feet, or affixed to their solid arms, they turn and record the people. From time to time, they pivot toward us, the audience. No matter what I do, it will be inscribed forever into their memories.

The man goes back down. Time passes.

My heart races. My stomach is empty and my chest is hollow. Even so, it's the only thing that matters. I am completely reliant on it. An empty chest that resounds with the beating of my heart.

It's our turn. The hand holding mine squeezes. It's our turn. Everything fades away. There's my chest, hers, and our hands. And the film that we made.

My chest, hers, our hands and the film.

My chest, hers, our hands and the film.

My chest, hers, our hands and our film.

I am pulled to the left and my body lifts.

It passes in front of the shifting knees.

It passes beneath my hair that falls over my face.

It passes beneath light applause.

It follows the black pants and the leather boots.

It moves through an aisle and arrives at the foot of the stairs.

It feels—in the audience—the vibrations of clapping hands.

My sandals guide me. They kiss the stairs, one after the other. Right cheek, left cheek. Right cheek again. They continue to follow the boots that don't seem to know the way anymore. Once on the stage, they go forward, to the right and then return to the left.

Then they stop suddenly, somewhere near the podium. We have arrived.

I see nothing in the theater. To the right, it's black. To the left, it's black. Above, blinding light. In front, I can't see the people. I hear only the growing applause.

Now, the hand of my friend. It is slender but firm. It trembles between my fingers, full and round.

I squeeze it. With all my hand's strength.

It cannot break. Her hand is slender but solid. She is slender but determined. She is slender but she brought us here.

She lets go of me. To take the prize—a glass sculpture—and to bring it slowly to her lips. And it quickly comes to rest on the podium, in front of her.

My friend talks, talks, talks. Like the first day we met. Even though I don't understand a word of what she's saying, I know that she's speaking fast. And I know that she's happy. Very happy. She says loads of things and I hear my name and Casablanca and my name again. She talks and she laughs.

And she gestures to me with the palm of her hand and the people applaud and they applaud and they applaud. And in the hall, I feel them stand as one.

And Chadlia looks at me, with the biggest smile I've seen since I met her. She smiles wider than her mouth. She smiles wider than her face. And her palm continues to gesture at me. And she pulls me toward the podium and she hands me the prize and it's heavy in my arms. I think I'm supposed to say something. The audience is still applauding. They are standing.

I have to say something.

Fuck, I have to say something.

Fucking fuck fuck, I have to say something.

"Uh... *Thank you.*"

They're still waiting. What on earth should I say to you?

"Uh... Thank you. Thank you. Thank you very much," I say into the microphone.

They're still standing and they keep going. They don't want to stop.

Something rises in me. I'm filling up. It moves through my feet like ants. And it accelerates. It climbs through my legs, it reaches my waist which swells beneath my belt. Now my chest. My chest fills with air. Air that sweeps through it like a tornado. I think it's joy.

In a surge, it's propelled to the sky. The air rises through my neck, it clears out my throat, it clarifies my voice, it penetrates my mouth, it awakens my tongue from its torpor, it spreads my lips. And, pure and clear and light as anything, arms open, it soars through my lips:

"*You you you you you you you you you you you you you you you you you you you you you you you you you you you you you you you you you you you you you you you you you you you you you you you you you you you you you you you you!*"

Epilogue

2018

May

"Jmiaa! Let's go!"

I don't have the strength to get up. This sun makes me dizzy. I think my last drink was one too many.

"Get up," says Samira.

"I can't," I sigh.

"Get up, that's enough!" she says to me.

"I'm telling you I can't," I continue, wiping my forehead, damp with sweat.

"I need something to help it all go down. I don't feel very well."

The sun is beating down right in my face. The street around us is lively. People come and go, everyone's busy with something.

"Fuck, you're so annoying," she says to me, getting up and turning her back to me.

And she adds:

"I'm leaving. I told your daughter I'd take her to buy some clothes."

Samira's yellow djellaba swishes: "Pft pft pft pft." She walks quickly and her hair scatters over either side of her neck.

On my right, I hear:

"*Liefje*, you're not feeling good?"

"I need that medicine you give me when the food doesn't want to stay down. My stomach is going to explode," I answer.

"Okay, I'll bring it to you."

Maaizou turns around and walks into the trailer to my right. It's only the third day of filming and I'm already tired. I think it's this heat.

I'm used to the sun and the heat but it's completely different in Mexico than in Morocco. When the sun beats down, it burrows into your brain until you can't tell what's going on around you anymore. To make things worse, we're filming outside today.

Usually, we're asleep at this hour, but both the scene we filmed yesterday and today's scene take place during the siesta. What can I do?

Drink lemonade, that's all there is to do. And with the lunches they give us, my stomach is as bloated as a goatskin. So I drink the baking soda concoction that Maaizou makes for me to help it go down.

Fortunately I don't drink alcohol anymore. It wouldn't have mixed well with the sun. Even when it's hot like this, honestly, there's nothing better than a nice cold beer that's sweating as much as you are.

But I promised: never again. I promised in front of that Doctor Fernando, who showed me the light, and I promised in front of myself in the mirror. "Never again will a drop of alcohol go down Jmiaa's throat. Never. Not in this world or in the next one."

It's hard. But what do you expect? If you want honey you have to put up with the bee sting.

It's been five years to the day since we won the prize, Chadlia and I. And since that day, everything's changed.

When I got back to Casablanca, a producer who had seen the film in America called Chadlia to tell her that he wanted to work with me. It had been three months since I returned, and I was already getting together my affairs and some money to emigrate secretly to America. After I won the prize, I was so happy that I couldn't wait to get back to Morocco to tell everyone about it. It wasn't until I arrived that I realized I had made a mistake and that I had to leave again.

And then, that guy called from out of nowhere. Rodrigo Buenavista is his name. He wanted to produce a new Mexican show with a Middle Eastern heroine.

The story is set in the previous century. There's a guy, the owner of a huge ranch, who travels to the desert and brings back a large brunette woman with immense eyes. A stereotypical chubby Arab woman, with long hair that she puts a lot of effort into.

Don Camillo—that's the hero—meets Oumaïma— that's me—and after many adventures, I'll tell you the details later, brings her back with him to Mexico. To his parents' house. They call it a hacienda here.

His entire family lives inside. His father, his mother, and his seven brothers and sisters. Including him, they're eight. Plus the servants and the farmhands and their children and even I can't keep track there are so many people.

Since Don Camillo is very rich and also the eldest son, his family has countless plans for him. His mother wants him to marry the daughter of her cousin. His father wants him to marry the daughter of the guy who owns the neighboring hills. His sister wants him to marry her best friend. Two of his brothers want to get rid of him so they can inherit the money instead. And so, when he brings me back as his wife, it creates even more of a mess in his crazy family. From that point on, the plot is to eliminate Oumaïma so they can get back to their original plans.

But my character, since she's clever, she dodges the strikes at every turn. Something unexpected happens in every episode. It's been on the air for three years. And every year, new things happen.

And since it's doing so well, it even airs in Morocco. Every day on Al Aoula at 2:30. There's not a person I know over there who doesn't watch. Hamid in his shed, the girls in their rooms, Abdelali at the restaurant, Okraïcha on the second floor, Mouy and her neighbors, my brothers and their wives...everyone. Even Chaïba, who's dropped his whore Hajar, watches, telling everyone—except his wife—that he and I were almost married.

And you know why it's so popular in our country? Because it's the first time that a Moroccan actress has had a part on a Mexican series.

Now when I go back, there are people who recognize me in the street. And when I arrive at the airport, Mouy gathers a welcome committee like no other. She brings bnader, my brothers, their wives, sometimes my cousins. They sing, they clap their hands, they yell youyous, as if I were coming back from the hajj. It's wonderful. Only Samia is bothered by it. She says it embarrasses her. But what can I say? She's fifteen years old now and that's a difficult age.

To tell the truth, it's the death of her father that really upset her. Even if she doesn't really remember him, she knew that she had a father somewhere in

Spain and that one day she would see him again. And last year—his first time back to Morocco since he left—the cursed man's bus flipped over between Tangier and Rabat. And he died inside. Isn't that shitty luck?

You know, despite everything, I cried. I didn't tell or show anyone, but I cried. The kid too, but that's normal.

The problem is that ever since, she hasn't really been herself. So to try to get her out of that state, I brought her Samira. I got her a passport and I brought her over. Given how well she took care of me when I was sick, I was sure there was no better person to keep Samia company while I worked. But she doesn't spend the entire year with us. Just six months out of the year. Because otherwise, she would need a visa and then it becomes complicated.

"Here, drink."

Maaizou hands me the glass of water mixed with the medicine. His face is red, like every day. He'll never adapt to this sun. He'll never tan like everyone else.

It's been two years since he joined me here, and for two years he's been roasting, the poor thing. But he doesn't complain. He never complains.

He's the same as he always was. Kind, carrying lights that weigh twice as much as him.

And now, he speaks Arabic almost as well as me.

For now, I don't speak any Dutch. The only thing I understand is *liefje*. That means "my little sweetheart." Or something like that.

In Spanish, they say *querida*. I know because their language entered my blood right away. If you heard me speak, you'd think I was one of them. Even better.

No one understands how I managed to learn so quickly.

Even though from the start I've been telling them that I'm sharp.

Glossary

Abdel Halim Hafez   Egyptian singer, lutist, and
actor of legendary renown in the 1950s and
'60s. He has such an iconic status in the Arab
world that he is typically referred to by just his
given name.

Aïcha Kandicha   A female jinn (spirit) who ap-
pears often in popular Moroccan mythology.
Some myths depict her as a demon with cloven
hooves, others as a witch, others as a spirit of
astounding beauty. All attest to her evil nature.

Aïn Diab   Literally, the "spring of wolves." A
beach in Casablanca.

Alpha 55   A shopping center in the heart of Casablanca's former European quarter. Because it's
been in existence for so long (it was built in
1979), it's become a local landmark.

Amr Diab   Egyptian singer popular in the 1990s; he was one of the first to combine Middle Eastern sounds with Western pop music. Also one of the first Arab pop idols for starry-eyed girls.

Anafa   Moroccan pronunciation of the French *en avant*, or "in front," used here to mean "Let's go."

Apaches of Raja   Along with Wydad, Raja is one of the two biggest soccer teams in Casablanca. Its most extreme fans are known for being particularly violent. The insult *awbach* (a rare classical Arabic word designating a type of insect, but commonly translated by Moroccans as "apaches") is often used in Morocco to describe hooligans, stemming from a speech by Hassan II in 1984. He used the term to describe rioters who had ransacked several cities to protest a hike in the price of bread.

Bac   Short for *baccalauréat*, an undergraduate degree.

Ba Lahcen Bechouia   "Go Slowly, Father Lahcen." A song by Haja El Hamdaouia, an obvious allusion to sex.

Bargache   Abderrahim Bargache, often designated by only his surname, presenter of a cooking show televised in the 1980s. As famous for his portliness as for his recipes.

Bimo   Brand of Moroccan cookies, now also used as a generic word for a cookie.

Bin-ou-bin "Between two."

Bismillah "In the name of God." Expression marking the beginning of everything in Muslim culture. In Morocco, "*dire bismillah*" means "begin."

Blue Bills The highest value of Moroccan bills is the two-hundred dirham note, which is blue and worth about 21 US dollars.

Bnader Plural of *bendir*: a drum traditionally fashioned from goatskin.

Caid A local official who serves as administrator, judge, and tax collector, all in one.

Chaabi Literally, "folk": used to describe folk music.

Cheikh Yassine The leader of a political and religious brotherhood whose full name was Abdesslam Yassine. He died in 2012.

Chemkara Feminine (or plural) of *chemkar*: a toothless beggar, generally covered in scars, addicted to psychotropic drugs or other hallucinogenic substances.

Chikhate Plural of *chikha*. Moroccan singers of satiric folk songs. Often plump, matronly women, they are sometimes associated with amorality or prostitution because of their free spirits and the boozy parties where they perform. They are in fact the guardians of a rich poetic heritage that Moroccans have recently begun to rediscover and celebrate with respect.

Choufi Ghirou, a l'azara 'ata Allah... "Find
yourself another man, there are plenty of single
guys." *Choufi ghirou* is the title of a famous song
by Najat Aatabou (see below).

Choumicha Host of successful cooking shows.

Cimi Adaptation of CMI, Compagnies mobiles
d'intervention, which are riot police.

Derb Omar A shopping district in Casablanca
that's mainly for wholesale purchases.

Fantasia An equestrian demonstration often performed as part of larger cultural performances.
It ends with the riders all shooting their guns
into the sky in unison.

Faqih A religious mystic, healer, fortune-teller, or
sorcerer—and often a mix of the four. The faqih
serves as "the people's shrink" in Morocco, and
interpreting dreams is one of his specialties.

Ghassoul Mineral clay, widely used by Moroccan
women to clean and care for their hair.

Grocery Store Berber grocery stores are often
used as informal networks for transferring
funds across the Mediterranean. The sender
gives dirhams to a grocer in Morocco, and the
recipient gets the equivalent in euros (minus
a commission) at the cousin's grocery store in
Europe—and vice versa.

Guerrab Clandestine seller of alcohol open late at night (official liquor stores close at eight o'clock).

Haja El Hamðaouia Famous Moroccan folk singer.

Hamðoullah "Thanks be to Allah."

Harira Thick soup made from tomatoes, flour, herbs, and starches.

Iftar Meal of the breaking of the daily fast during Ramadan. The same word is used for breakfast.

Ilyeh Moroccan pronunciation of the French phrase "il y est," shouted to celebrate a soccer goal, generally by overexcited fans.

Imað Ntifi Famous presenter of musical and other entertainment shows.

Jðiða El Jadida, a port town about sixty miles south of Casablanca.

Jmiaa Bent Larbi "Jmiaa, daughter of Larbi."

Kaaba Black cubic building located at the center of the Great Mosque of Mecca. The Kaaba is literally the epicenter of Islam. Circling the Kaaba seven times is the principle rite performed by Muslims when they make their pilgrimage to Mecca.

Lebssa Traditional Moroccan outfit, often very colorful, worn by women for important occasions like marriages, baptisms, and other ceremonies.

Lhajja Feminine form of *Hajji*, the title accorded to those who have completed the pilgrimage to Mecca. Also commonly used to refer respectfully to an elderly woman.

Maaizou "Little goat." A familiar expression, halfway between mockery and affection, to refer to someone who is fairly puny but gifted with a special touch.

Maallem Master artisan, although the term is used to refer to anyone who masters a profession or a particular skill, as a mark of recognition of their talent.

Maâmora Forest of cork oaks in the Rabat region covering more than 150,000 acres.

Maârif Shopping district in Casablanca, home to numerous stores and cafés. Also a flirting hot spot: boys and girls hang out there on weekends, dressed in the latest fashions.

Men Dar Ldar "From house to house."

Mkharka A honey cake traditionally prepared for Ramadan, served alongside harira (see above).

Moqaddem Agent of the Ministry of the Interior. At the bottom of the administrative ladder, he is in charge of direct contact with the population—a job that is often turned into a source of profit.

Moqataa   District headquarters, the local administration in charge of birth certificates, proof of residences, and other official documents.

Moukhtafoune   Television series devoted to finding missing persons.

Moussem   One of the annual regional festivals that combine the celebration of local saints with shopping, amusement park rides, and large-scale public entertainment, such as folk troupe concerts and fantasias.

Mouy   My mother.

Msemen   Pancake made from puff pastry.

Najat Aatabou   Internationally famous Moroccan folk singer. Called "the lioness of the Atlas," she sings about the struggle for women in a chauvinistic society and embodies a bold folk feminism free of inhibitions.

Nancy Ajram   Lebanese pop music singer, as famous for her plunging necklines as for her love songs.

Nass El Ghiwane   A legendary Moroccan musical group popular in the 1970s for their political and poetic lyrics, as well as their revolutionary rhythms. Martin Scorsese once called them the "Rolling Stones of Africa."

Nassima el Hor   Famous host of discussion shows about social issues. Because of her great empathy for those in the lower classes, many of them consider her the quintessence of journalism.

Okraïcha Literally, "the witch."

Pepitas Sunflower or pumpkin seeds that are grilled and salted. Peeling and eating pepitas is done in a characteristic gesture displaying dexterity and practice, often engendering an intensive idleness. A highly addictive activity, it is also ideal for walks with friends or solitary contemplation of the street.

Rfissate (plural of *rfissa*) A festive dish made from chicken, msemen, fenugreek, and lentils, traditionally prepared for a newborn child.

Rial From the Spanish *real*, currency formerly used in the north of Morocco under Spanish occupation. The currency is no longer in use today, but some prices are still quoted in rials, especially by those in the lower classes. One thousand rials is worth roughly $5, or 50 dirhams, the current Moroccan currency (1 dirham = 20 rials).

Robio A nickname for redheads in Morocco. From the Spanish *rubio*.

Sanicroix Brand of household cleaner, and a generic name given to all floor-cleaning products.

Selham Long men's cape, generally white, worn for important occasions over a djellaba.

Semsara Feminine of *semsar*, an intermediary who facilitates a transaction in order to procure a good (for instance, lodging or an automobile) or a service (such as maid recruitment or an administrative affair), in exchange for a commission. The *smasria* (plural of *semsar*) are often hired on café terraces, and always work informally. Those specializing in placing maids are generally women.

Shah Rukh Khan Indian star of Bollywood films that are immensely popular in Morocco.

Si Mohamed Generic name used for a stranger.

Sirwal Loose-fitting pants with a distinctively wide crotch that reaches the knees.

Siviana Moroccan pronunciation of "Sévillane," a brand of cheap tinned sardines that are very popular in the country.

Tabac: A tobacco store that also sells items such as newspapers, phone cards, and stamps, and is often a bar as well.

Thirty-Six Psychiatric care unit located near Berrechid, approximately twenty-two miles south of Casablanca.

Twin Short for "Twin Center," a shopping center at the foot of the two twin towers at the entrance of the Maârif neighborhood in Casablanca.

Wilaya Prefecture. The wali, the highest authority in the wilaya, is an important figure in Morocco.

Zellige Moroccan-style tiles, often laid in intricate patterns.

Meryem Alaoui was born and raised in Morocco, where she managed an independent media group that combined publications in French (*TelQuel*) and Arabic (*Nichane*). *Straight from the Horse's Mouth*, her debut novel, was first published in France, where it has achieved great critical acclaim. After several years in New York, Alaoui now lives in Morocco.

Emma Ramadan is a literary translator based in Providence, Rhode Island, where she co-owns Riffraff bookstore and bar. She is the recipient of an NEA Translation Fellowship, a PEN/Heim Translation Fund grant, a Fulbright, and the 2018 Albertine Prize. Her translations include *Sphinx* and *Not One Day* by Anne Garréta, *Pretty Things* by Virginie Despentes, *The Shutters* by Ahmed Bouanani, and *Me & Other Writing* by Marguerite Duras.

ꙮ OTHER PRESS

You might also enjoy these titles from our list:

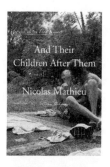

AND THEIR CHILDREN AFTER THEM
by Nicolas Mathieu

Winner of the 2018 Prix Goncourt, this poignant coming-of-age tale captures the distinct feeling of summer in a region left behind by global progress.

"[A] page-turner…As suffused with local color as this book is, parallels with left-behind swaths of America stand out on every page…It is easy to see why this novel…would find such critical acclaim… I couldn't put the book down. I didn't want it to end." —*New York Times Book Review*

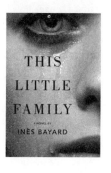

THIS LITTLE FAMILY by Inès Bayard

This striking debut novel inhabits the mind of a young married woman driven to extremes by disgust and dread in the aftermath of a rape.

"[A] stunning debut…with a defiant, feral energy that has echoes of Elena Ferrante's *Days of Abandonment*…a powerful study of sexual violence and its aftermath." —*Publishers Weekly* (starred review)

WOMEN by Mihail Sebastian

A rediscovered classic from the author of *For Two Thousand Years*, this remarkable novel offers surprisingly modern portraits of romantic relationships in the early twentieth century, from unrequited loves and passionate affairs to tepid marriages of convenience.

"A compelling portrait of desire in its many convoluted manifestations." —*Kirkus Reviews*

Additionally recommended:

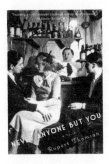

NEVER ANYONE BUT YOU by Rupert Thomson

NAMED A BEST BOOK OF THE YEAR BY *THE GUARDIAN, THE OBSERVER,* AND *SYDNEY MORNING HERALD*

A literary tour de force that traces the real-life love affair of two extraordinary women, recreating the surrealist movement in Paris and the horrors of war.

"There's so much sheer moxie, prismatic identity, pleasure, and danger in these lives...the scenes are tense, particular, and embodied...wonderfully peculiar." —*New York Times Book Review*

PAIN by Zeruya Shalev

A powerful, astute novel that exposes how old passions can return, testing our capacity to make choices about what is most essential in life.

"Shalev reminds readers in keen, often brilliant prose that love, like pain, is indelible...a riveting exploration of family, sex, and motherhood." —*New York Times Book Review*

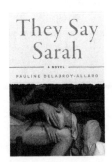

THEY SAY SARAH by Pauline Delabroy-Allard

A literary sensation in France, this poetic, thrilling debut charts the all-consuming passion between two women and the ruin it leaves in its wake.

"This poetic and mystifying debut draws blood." —*New York Times Book Review*

"Titillating with its frank descriptions of sex...and captivating with its investigation of the suffering involved in passion. It's a brief, intense read... alluring and disturbing." —*The Guardian*

OTHER PRESS

www.otherpress.com